ALL RIGHTS RESERVED
No part of this book may be reproduced or transmitted in
any form or by any means, electronic or mechanical,

including photocopying, recording, or by any information storage
and retrieval system, without permission in writing from the author except in the case of brief quotations embodied in reviews.
Publisher's Note:
This is a work of fiction,
the work of the author's imagination.
Any resemblance to real persons or events is coincidental.

Copyright September 2021 – Ana Calin

Table of Contents

Copyright Page 1
CHAPTER I 4
CHAPTER II 31
CHAPTER III 49
CHAPTER IV 68
CHAPTER V 90
CHAPTER VI 118
THE END 125

CHAPTER I

Edith

HERE WE ARE AGAIN, Sandros Nightfrost and I. Right back where we started, with my puppy brown eyes raised to his beastly golden irises as we face each other across the table. He's as heartbreakingly unattainable as he was years ago, when I was first placed under his protective wing. Or, more accurately, in his power. After all, he was the "master" and I his servant, even if it was on a battlefield where we acted as one, telepathically bonded.

Things have changed since then. A lot.

Now I'm the lady of a French chateau, the trophy wife of Lord Durion Mithriel for all the town's high society is concerned. To them, I'm an ethereal blonde with waves of white-blonde hair cascading down her back, always dressed in designer clothes and a bit drunk. I play the part best with a glass of champagne in my hand at social functions. I never actually drink it, but no one ever notices. As long as it suits the image they've made of me, my true identity is safe.

The opulence of my dresses and jewelry is also necessary. The physical appearance of the fae is unusual for humans, and believe it or not, the best way to keep suspicion at bay is by flaunting it. People often refer to this effect as 'surreal beauty,' even though I personally don't consider us more beautiful than humans. We're just more like what they desire for themselves. So Durion and I freely display the luxury we live in, our expensive clothing, the cars, the chateau. This way, people just assume we 'bought' our looks too—expensive face creams, the best pills, the right surgeons, some even consider bioengineering. I heard them whispering at the last function we attended.

We also have to display a relationship that doesn't actually exist. Though we play the married couple, in the months Durion and I have been exiled here in the human realm I've come to loathe him. He treats me like his possession, and there's always an undertone of menace in his communication toward me. But I have no choice but to put up with him, otherwise I know he's got ways to hurt me.

Sandros doesn't know all this, of course. He doesn't know that the closeness between Durion and me is a ruse. He didn't give me the opportunity to explain, neither the first time we saw each other at the mayor's birthday party two days ago, nor during the two minutes we had to ourselves in this room before Durion stepped in, stiff and square-shouldered like a royal rooster with his full head of golden curls and his chest pumped forward. He's come to take this charade of the two of us being a married couple of noblemen dangerously seriously and now, as we sit here across from Sandros, he seems more committed to it than ever. The possibility of his sliding his hand under the table on my thigh hovers like a dark cloud over my head. It's a possibility that Sandros feels, too.

Despite Sandros' hostility towards me, our bond is still there. It's an inescapable connection, one that he obviously hates being tangled in. He doesn't love me, while I always have loved him, ever since the very beginning, even as he treated me like shit.

Because I'm an idiot like that.

This time Sandros doesn't face us as the army general that everyone used to fear, the beast in studded leather armor that every woman at the winter court secretly wanted to fuck but would never dream of admitting it. No, this time he's sitting across from us in a fitted suit that wraps his body in a mouthwatering way, his look classy but also wild with his sharply chiseled face and long black hair. No wonder the plates clatter on the server girls' trays as they scurry around with starters and drinks.

"So, you're telling me that Nessima sent you here to speak to her benefactor on her behalf," Durion says, his face filled with suspicion. "I'm sorry, but I find that highly improbable."

"What's so hard to believe about it?" Sandros rumbles, his voice like low thunder.

"You stayed back at her estate as her prisoner. Two months later you emerge as her right hand? I'm sorry, but it doesn't make sense."

"I found a way into her heart, and from there, into her trust."

I fidget in my seat. Bastard must know he just plunged a knife into my heart.

"We're together now," he twists the knife. "I'm sure that, if you think about it, it'll make sense that she'd let me handle some of her more serious affairs."

"As I am sure you understand my reservations. This isn't some Shanghai CEO that she sent you to meet, it's not Bill Gates or the President. It's the fucking Antichrist." Durion's last word makes me flinch, which isn't lost on Sandros. His golden eyes move between Durion and me as Durion places a hand over mine.

"It's taken Nessima centuries to gain access to him," Durion continues. "It seems unlikely to me that she should share that power, no matter how in love she is. Especially after what happened with her first husband."

"Officially, Eldan Blackfall is still her husband."

"So, the two of you can't *really* be together?" Durion says. "And yet she's given you more power than she ever even took for herself? Come on."

"She actually asked me nicely to take it," Sandros rumbles, his golden eyes glinting like honey and hellfire. "As a warrior, I have a reputation. She wanted that reputed skill and influence on her side."

That sounds so true it cuts yet deeper.

My pulse rises to the point that I can't breathe. It's hard to put up with the tension between the two men, and even harder to withstand the waves of hostility that hit me from Sandros. I'm painfully focused on his presence, and I can't shake it. Everything seems to fade around him, even this chateau with its paneled walls and luxury fittings.

There's no comfort in the expensively upholstered chairs or the intricately carved ornaments of the great fireplace, not even in the intimate light of the candelabra, or the statues and expensive art surrounding us.

The flames from the fireplace cast a golden light on the sharp angles of Sandros' face, licking his caramel-bronze skin. Maybe I've lived among humans for too long, and gotten so used to their appearances, that this fae warlord now seems as surreal to me as he does to them. Even looking at him hurts.

"Suppose we believe you, Edith and I," Durion tells him. "Say we accept that Nessima sent you here to act on her behalf. Did she give you his identity then? Because we've been here for months, and still haven't gotten the slightest clue. It could be anyone from the town mayor to the baker."

"Yes. I do know who it is."

My breath stops, my eyes enlarging in shock.

"You do?" I whisper.

"Yes. But, unfortunately, I cannot share that information with you." His gaze brushes unwillingly over to me. "Either one of you."

A server enters, awkward on her feet, the china clattering on her tray. It must be Sandros' handsomeness that's gotten her all flustered, because it couldn't be the topic of our conversation. We're speaking winter fae language, which resembles human English, but she doesn't understand that one very well either.

"I'm here because Nessima needs more of his support, and she thinks he would grant it to me easier than to her. There are things that I can offer him, and she can't. Things are also becoming urgent because, ever since her husband Eldan came out of the coma, the King has been planning an invasion of the North, intent on crushing her forces. She will rely on her benefactor more than ever."

"And may I ask how Eldan has been cleansed of the evil that kept him unconscious?" Durion pushes. "We all know that Nessima implanted it into him, and only she could get it out of his system."

Sandros raises his square chin.

"I persuaded Nessima to retract it from him."

Durion throws his head back, letting out a fake laugh. "Really now? And all that only through your talents as a lover?"

"I offered her my complete allegiance in return. My unwavering loyalty."

"And she believed you?" I chime in, pressing the lid down on my boiling feelings.

Sandros stares at me, and it feels like a damned train crash.

"That's where my talents as a lover came into play."

And, with that, the knife tears deeper into my flesh.

It's obvious that Sandros isn't here only a mission, he's also back to torture me. It seemed surreal that he should have turned on the King of Winter, his own half-brother that he served for centuries upon centuries until this woman Nessima came along and screwed up our lives, but apparently it's true. So true that the blood drains from my head.

How could he? How could he betray the king, and more yet, how could he betray *me*? We're bonded mates, and that's something almost impossible to break. But this bond feels different for Sandros than it does for me, and if I'm completely honest with myself, deep down, I always knew. When he first took me in that storeroom under the stairs at Nessima's estate, I knew I was doomed. I'll always want this warlord, while he'll always find reasons to despise me. As intense as our sex was, as deep our connection, it was about love to me, and about possession and power to him.

"Now here's how things are going to go down," Sandros says, broadening his shoulders. "I'm going to contact *him*, but that will have to be in a crowd, because a crowd is what best confers anonymity. So, let's start by making a list of upcoming events and, if there aren't any, we'll set up one ourselves."

"Why would we help you?" I bite out, defiance heating my eyeballs. "You're betraying your brother the King of Winter, and everyone you professed to care about by doing this. All this means we're not on the same side anymore—doesn't it, Durion?"

Durion blinks and babbles a little before he replies, "Why yes, yes, of course, yes."

It must come as a shock to him that I'm putting us in the same boat, him and me, but he likes it, I can tell. It softens him toward me and the entire situation, which is good, because even though I loathe him, I need all the allies I can get right this moment, since I feel like I'm going to hell.

The hint of this new alliance isn't lost on Sandros either, who assesses us for a few moments before a wicked grin quirks up his chiseled, forbidden-fruit of a mouth. He leans forward, slowly, placing his elbows on the table, seeming even bigger, his shadow growing over the curtains behind him in the firelight. Durion stiffens in his seat, his shoulders and jaw clenching as he tries to hang on to his resistant attitude.

"The two of you make one hell of a pair," Sandros slurs.

I don't respond. Let's see just how far Sandros' rotten opinion of me can go.

"You will help me because you have no choice," he eventually says, pushing his chair back. When he rises, he does it like a gliding python.

I watch him as he prowls over to the fireplace. The sleek suit doesn't do anything to mask his feral nature, on the contrary, it works as an enhancement. He picks a red rose from a gilded holder on the mantelpiece, pushing his free hand into his pocket. The suit tightens on his arm, sending a flash of memory involving those arms around me, subduing me.

I shake my head to cast out the memory that threatens to spread through me like a disease.

"These look like they are more than just decoration." His voice is as controlled as ever, but I can feel the poison behind it. I hold back from probing his mind telepathically, because he would feel me there, and I'm not sure I want to know the full extent of his resentment. "Are red roses a regular gift in this place?"

"I've spared no effort to make Edith's exile in the human realm as pleasant as possible."

"Oh, but being in the human realm has hardly ever been torture for her," Sandros rumbles, his tone lashing. "Let me remind you her illegally crossing over into the human realm and screwing human boys was the reason she got thrown in the Ice King's dungeon in the first place."

"Come on, Sandros, that was ages ago," I burst out. "I've paid for my mistakes, I was locked down for years, and then I served you in the war against the Lord of Fire. Sure, the stigma never went away, it might never go away, but I won't have you judging me, not anymore."

Durion places a long-fingered hand on my shoulder, and this time I don't shake it off. Two servers enter with the last of the tableware and make to take positions by the door, standing in expectation to wait on us, but Sandros has other plans.

"Thank you very much for everything," he tells them in a deep voice that makes the blood surge into the women's cheeks. They're so affected by him their thoughts are senseless clamor in my ears. "You can leave now. Take the night off. Actually, take tomorrow too. Tell the rest of the staff, it's whole free week for everybody."

The two women look at each other, and then at Durion and me. I can feel his thoughts, he's furious that Sandros should take upon himself to give our staff orders, but he knows that clearing the chateau of personnel is the right thing to do. The *safe* thing to do. We nod at the women, and watch them reluctantly leave. Their thoughts still echo inside my skull, and I can make out some sense in them—they'd love to stay, find out more about the mysterious visitor. One of them particularly likes having his eyes on her, it stimulates her sexual fantasy in which he's forcing her down to her knees, fist clenched in her hair. She wonders if he's married, but doesn't seem to care even if that's the case.

"I quit judging you a long time ago, Edith," Sandros addresses me as soon as the servers have cleared the room. "I think by now we know each other well enough to know what to expect."

"Believe it or not, I would very much prefer to return to the Winter Realm," I say. "To the Queen, who I'm honored to call my best friend, and to the King, who happens to be your half-brother." I stick out my chin. "I guess I don't know you as well as you assume. I would have never expected you to switch sides. To cross to Nessima Blackfall's side, no less, the woman who tried to kill your best friend Eldan in punishment for having found the love of his life in a man instead of her. You've turned your back on all the centuries that you and the King have fought side by side? And for what? Pussy?" I scoff.

It's satisfying to hold the words on my tongue like that. He sure didn't expect that kind of reaction from me, and on the one hand it felt good. But on the other it feels like I've just drunk poison because I'm putting things into a perspective that's hard as Tartarus to bear. But since he's determined to think the worst of me, I might as well return in kind.

Yes, years ago I found a way to slip into the human realm and have fun at frat parties. I had my first lover there, but I wasn't doing it with "boys". It was only one boy, and Sandros knows that. When we connected, current running through us, creating the mates' bond, he saw the guy with the number eight on the back of his jacket.

"I'm not here to explain my motives to you." His tone is flat as if my words had bounced against a wall. "I'm here to let you know how things are going to go down. So—"

"We don't need to make a list of events," I cut him off. "There's enough high society in this town that there's always something going on. There was the mayor's birthday two days ago, and there's the engagement of Count Guerin's son on Saturday. He's celebrating at the same restaurant as the mayor—the medieval tower on the hill, the best place in all the region."

"Not going to have every person in town there, though," Durion argues. "It's going to be only the high society, so the person you expect to meet there—"

"The high society is all we need," Sandros declares.

"So, then we know the Antichrist is a member," Durion says under his breath.

"Not surprised." I pick up the bottle of champagne and pour myself a drink, refusing Durion's attempt at helping with one forbidding look that he doesn't challenge. He hasn't seen this side of me before, and that takes him a little off balance. Quite frankly, I don't know myself like this either. "Who would imagine the devil's very son wandering the world in a state of poverty or even merely as someone mediocrely well-off?"

"The Antichrist came here to enjoy the good life, that's for sure," Sandros says. I feel his eyes on me as

I keep pouring champagne into my glass. I do it slowly, watching the liquid glisten and the foam swell, tilting the glass to prolog the process.

"Who's on the guest list?" Sandros goes on.

I leave the replying to Durion, downing my champagne and letting my eyes wander over Sandros' frame.

Will I ever be free from his spell, or am I doomed to die under it, like all the other disposable women that came before me in his life? When Sandros Nightfrost chooses to unleash his masculine talents on a woman, it's not long until she becomes his emotional slave, just like I've become. No doubt in the months we've been apart he's made an adoring idiot out of Nessima. By Tartarus, I wish that the champagne could give me the slightest high, I'm in desperate need of it. But nothing but a particular kind of fae nectar is going to do *that* trick.

"Listen, Sandros," I interrupt. "Any chance you brought along some nectar?"

He cocks an eyebrow inquisitively.

"It was the last of my concerns, but I'm sure I can arrange something for you, *if* you work with me now. Let's get back to our business at hand, and talk contraband later."

So the bastard's going to make me work for it.

"All right, so the engagement party," Durion resumes, probably spurred on by my playing myself on his side earlier.

But I'll be damned. I can't wrap my head around the fact that Sandros is here to betray his brother the King of Frost after so many centuries in which they'd been so close one could have sworn they were

Siamese twins. I can't believe he's aiding Nessima and the Antichrist in taking over the Winter Realm.

Durion pushes his chair back, the wooden legs scraping the floor, and walks around the table to Sandros, who watches him with hawkish eyes.

"There are a few people of note in this town, and they like to be around each other, you know, they feel safer that way. The rich don't despise the poor as much as they fear they'd kill them for the crumbs from their tables."

"I didn't come here for philosophy," Sandros cuts him off. Durion wants to retort something ugly, but refrains. I can feel the fuel behind his friendliness is the newly awakened hopes that he has with me now, damn it.

"The mayor isn't the most important person in this place," he continues, picking up an oyster and slurping on it, while Sandros leans with his shoulder against the wall, the flames dancing in his golden eyes.

"Guerin the Count de Auvergne is the oldest and most respected citizen here. A number of mayors showered him with distinctions over the years. From what I gather he played a huge part against Hitler, but he's too old now to play a part in anything remotely challenging. He's extremely well connected though, and he's trying hard to pass his connections on to his son, Antoine. Except skill and life experience isn't passed on as easily as money, and Antoine's turning out a good-for-nothing that's squandering his father's inheritance before the old man's even in the ground isn't making it any easier. He's a drunk, an addict, and a womanizer.

"Guerin has started to see that Antoine has anything but a bright future ahead of him once the old man's dead, so he's trying to save the situation through an arranged marriage. The engagement party between Antoine de Auvergne and Simone Carrera is thus based on anything but love. She's not a noblewoman, but she's rich, an heiress. Used to be a great beauty, and she's still attractive, by human standards, even though she's got her best years behind her. So, she could still have her choice of men, easily, so old Guerin has to make the union interesting for her, and especially, profitable. They must have stricken a good deal. She's very savvy in the business area, I've heard."

Has the champagne started to have an effect, or is Sandros glancing at me every other sentence?

"So these three will be the main people at the engagement party on Saturday, but there will also be the mayor, Jean Dubois. He's a cliché-ish middle aged politician pervert that won't miss a chance to hover around Giancarlo Botini, a fashion designer who's not *entirely* cliché." He glances at me with hidden meaning. "He's extravagant, dark sunglasses at midnight and such, but he's as into women as it gets. Most of all into Edith."

Sandros' eyes fly over to me, the complete mirror of Durion's, except there's also some sort of reproach in there, as if I'm to blame for the attention.

"Come on Durion, what he wants is for me to model for him," I counter, even though I hate it that I want to set Sandros' opinion straight. "To him, I'm the stereotypical trophy wife with an alcohol problem and good legs. He just thinks I'd look good on a catwalk."

"Which you most certainly would," Durion says. "But the truth is, Sandros, it's not only the pretty trophy wife that Botini sees. As a fae, I have no doubt Edith is the most beautiful woman he's ever seen. Unless, of course, he is the Antichrist, and he's seen this kind of supernatural beauty before."

Sandros walks around him as if he's heard everything he needed to hear. "So, all these people are going to be at the engagement party."

"Them and more." Durion spins on his heel to face Sandros' back as the latter walks a shirt distance away. "The mayor's connections, high-flying politicians and corporate sharks, also the more important part of his extended family will be there. The mayor also has two sons from a surrogate mother, but I suppose they're irrelevant."

"Now why would you suppose that?"

"What do you mean why? They're toddlers. Twins."

Pretty weird looking twins, if you ask me, but I could still kiss and pinch those doughy cheeks. They're chubby, and sweet, and yet I can understand people's reluctance to go anywhere near them. They have disturbingly wiry copper hair and uncomfortably piercing blue eyes that would make the night unsettling for the most settled of minds. Human minds. Not used to facing demons and dragon shifters in battle, oblivious to the incredible worlds existing around their own.

"It's decided, then," Sandros states matter-of-factly, placing the rose slowly on the table right across from me. "We'll be attending that engagement party on Saturday, and you will be introducing me as your distant cousin."

Our eyes meet, and his nail me to the chair. Durion can't catch the look between us, since Sandros has his back at him, and I manage to suppress any reaction that threatens to move a muscle on my face.

"And by what name should I introduce you?" Durion says. "Because I can't possibly use your real one. These are generations' old noblemen and politicians and corporate moguls, they'll know—"

"They'll know I'm someone they've never heard of, and yet someone with enough power to infiltrate their ranks. Someone that looks different enough to raise their curiosity. When these things awaken curiosity, respect tends to follow. It will open all the doors that need to be opened."

Silence falls over the room, only the fire's rustling filling the air, the flames bathing the place in a timeless light. I like it because it reminds me of my old world, of my true home in the Winter Realm. The Snowstorm estate, the abandoned fortress of my family. It's now probably infested with Nessima's dark power, since her evil has gaped to swallow the entire territory beyond the Northern Forest.

"I'll be staying in the east wing. Tell the staff not to venture there. I understand it's still undergoing renovation anyway," Sandros declares, turning to leave.

"The renovations have only just started," Durion corrects him. "It's actually in a pretty bad state right now, it's hardly a proper lodging for—"

"I've had worse. I spent half of my life in war camps. I'll be fine."

"Can't say the betrayal wasn't expected," Durion says when we're alone again, his eyes still fixed on the archway through which Sandros has just exited. He pours himself a glass of champagne, and downs it in one go. Alcohol doesn't have an effect on either of us, but the prickling, fine taste of French booze can be soothing. "You should have known, too. He's the son of the former winter king and a powerful demoness from Hell. Evil has always coursed through his veins, that's why our people have always been instinctively wary of him."

"You're right."

For a moment, Durion looks like he's about to slap himself. "Wait, you actually agree with me about him? What's the catch?"

"No catch. It's the way it is. Pour me some, too." I wave my hand to the bottle, slouching back in my seat. I must look a hot mess. My dress is off the shoulder, which I guess adds to my overall desolate appearance as I let a man I loathe fill my glass instead of the one I want, who left the room without giving me another glance. I keep staring at the rose he placed in front of me, which has already started to wilt, blackening under his dark power.

"I don't think you've ever agreed with me on anything before," Durion says as the champagne gurgles into the glass.

"I'd be an idiot to not agree with you on this one. But agreeing isn't going to get us anywhere." I meet Durion's eyes as I replay the evening in my head. "The realms are in mortal danger again. The

Antichrist is here, in the human world, the centerpiece that holds all the worlds together. And now, the darkest prince of the Winter Realm has joined him. If these two come together, the worlds are going to collapse, and evil is going to swallow us all."

Durion nods, dread starting to spread in his large brown eyes. "We have to do something."

"First of all, we have to find out who the Antichrist is."

Edith

"HOW WAS IT?" CALLIE says as she barges into my room. "Seeing him after all this time?"

I'm still staring out the window, bracing myself, as if that could protect me against my own intoxicating emotions.

I sink my head, my shoulders slouching. "I'm still weak at the knees."

I don't have to pretend with Callie. I can't stop thinking about him, wondering what he thinks about me, if he has at least an ounce of affection left. If he even still sees me as a woman. But, no matter how hard I try, I can't imagine a version of the universe in which he feels about me the way I feel about him.

"What about him? How did he react when he saw you? These bonds go both ways, you know."

It's like she read my mind, but sadly the only mind reader here is me. Callie is a healer. She can work well with herbs, while I can work well with people's minds. One peek would tell me what Sandros feels for me, but no. Most likely what I'm going to find in there is his feelings for Nessima, memories of him thrusting into her, the sound of her moans attacking my ears. No, probing Sandros' mind could prove poison for my heart.

"It would be wishful thinking to say he still wanted me. If anything, he hates my guts. He thinks I've given myself to Durion." It hurts even as I say it.

"Well, then tell him the truth," she says as I turn around, hands on her hips. "Tell him it's only a ruse for the town's members, and—"

"I can't. You know what Durion said, everybody is to think our relationship is real, *absolutely* everybody, and now that I've seen Sandros again, I think that's actually a good idea. He appears to be on the devil's side now." I look into her large green eyes that have intrigued everyone who ever saw them, not least because of their sheer size on her small, sweet face. "I don't dare cross either Durion or Sandros at this time. They could both prove dangerous, not only to me, but also you. And I couldn't bear anything happening to you." It would be the last blow, I would collapse. And I can't afford to collapse, not now.

"Which I deeply appreciate, you know that. But this is Sandros, your true mate, he can help—"

"It doesn't matter," I stop her, more abruptly than I intended. "Think about it. Isn't it odd that Nessima should suddenly give him the freedom to turn up here when the reason she exiled Durion and me in the human realm in the first place was to separate us? Something's not right. I don't trust Sandros any more than Durion does. And besides, he became Nessima's lover, probably very soon after I left. He admitted it himself, with his head up no less, but he wants to punish *me* for being with Durion. You know what, no! I'm no longer the convict girl, the slave that was placed at his disposal during the war to help him through her telepathic abilities. I'm my own woman now."

"But—"

"There's more," I cut her off. "The bond that we share. He could try and probe my mind, find out the truth about Durion and me. I wouldn't even have to tell him. But no, he *wants* to believe I'm a dirty little whore, doesn't he? He likes believing that because it gives him the right to treat me like shit, and if there's anything Sandros enjoys beyond measure, it's to treat me like shit. But not this time, I won't let him."

I make a decision for myself that pours like acid on my heart, but it's necessary acid.

"If he's going to believe the worst about me anyway, I might as well let him. I've been trying too hard to persuade him of my virtues, and I only ended up looking stupid."

"None of that means that he doesn't feel your bond deeply. Maybe he's just dissimulating, he's good at that." Callie sits down beside me on the bed. She holds up her finger as if the greatest idea just hit her. "You say he didn't bother to probe your mind, but he could say the same about you. So why don't you take the first step?"

I let out a laugh that sounds as bitter as the taste of his betrayal. "And dabble in his feelings for Nessima, maybe watch him fucking her for a few torturous moments? I wouldn't be able to get out of his mind fast enough." I push myself off the bed and walk back to the window, my naked feet hitting the hem of my vaporous dress in which I feel like a wretched princess. I've been using human make-up lately, too, and now that I see my dim reflection in the window pane, I feel quite the part of the scorned woman with the smudged mascara around my eyes, and the dress hanging loosely off one round, ghostly shoulder like I've torn my clothes in despair.

I would look a mess for the fae, especially to Sandros, but for humans, I would still draw much unwanted attention. My face is unnaturally young for a woman with white hair, but I suppose that's part of my allure to humans. It's part of what fascinates them, the dichotomy of young and old, and the contrast between the signs of emotional decay and a fresh face they consider so very desirable.

I don't think I've ever been looked at with as much lecherous craving as I have been ogled by the human men here. Rich privilege is a very real thing in the human realm because, unlike supernaturals, humans are wounded creatures that seek to fill the void inside with money, booze, drugs, cigarettes, sex. They gorge themselves on all that poison until their bodies look like shit, and then they struggle to prove to themselves they're still worthy of love and respect through more excess.

Rich men will cheat on their wives with younger women. Often, they'll take new, beautiful wives as if that foreign beauty could compensate for their own deformed appearance, which they often have no one but their own decadent lifestyle to blame for. But the models are never enough to fill that void either, so the men end up consuming them one after the other, never reaching that sense of satiation that they're so ravenously searching for.

The void stays. For both sides involved.

The case of Antoine de Auvergne, the man whose engagement we're supposed to celebrate on Saturday, is no different. The son of Count Guerin de Auvergne is a thirty-year-old drunk who's already balding, he's skinny but with the big gut that I've come to recognize as specific to alcoholics, and his shirt is as good as always open to reveal a hairy and always sweaty chest. He's got nice face features, though, probably looking more like his mother than his father. He also gets sleazy rather quickly, no more than three drinks in, and often he does indeed seem to become a whole new, highly disgusting person.

He's quiet and often sulking when he's sober, but way too bold when he's drunk, when security often ends up holding him back from wreaking havoc. A few times the police had to take action, but old Guerin paid them off.

He still has power and influence, the old man, even from his wheelchair. Durion thinks his connections will soon dwindle, but to me he seems to grow more powerful by the day. Of course, I don't know how things were back in his fifties and sixties, when he was still big and strong, but now, in his eighties, the shriveled old man in the wheelchair seems to cast a shadow that could crush everyone around him.

Even the mayor Jean Dubois and his favorite boy the fashion designer Giancarlo Botini are intimidated, even though an air of dark secret surrounds them, too. It's safe to say Botini is the most handsome man in town, and he invests a lot of money to ensure he maintains that image, but his aura is tainted. The aura is inescapable for humans, and it only changes when they change on the inside. But Giancarlo hasn't changed since he's done whatever terrible thing that damaged his aura like that.

None of it shows in his physical appearance, though. Black hair gelled back, eyes hidden behind permanent sunglasses, well worked-out body and permanently open shirt to reveal tattooed, perfectly lean muscles, he's the complete opposite of Antoine de Auvergne. The mayor, a middle-aged man you'd never guess is gay, has been into him for all the time we've known him.

Giancarlo has little talent but a lot of money, because he knows how to manipulate people to get his way, including Mr. Mayor. I have a hunch the mayor has been sponsoring him for a long time in the hopes that he'd get at least a night of passion with the designer, but that's never going to happen. Giancarlo has only been leading Jean Dubois on because, in truth, he is a ladies' man.

And now he's got his sights set on me.

I've tried to discover the Antichrist's identity ever since I got here, but such a mind would be bulletproof. There's no way to probe deep enough. Put simply, I'm not strong enough to get inside the Antichrist's mind, and all of these people have a deeply dark side to them that I can only penetrate this far without damage. Fact is, it could be anyone.

I stare out the window at the wide landscape of green hills, fog shrouding them. It's a beautiful sight, even if a little unsettling. There's something almost magical about it, and it's full of places that remind me strongly of the supernatural realms, especially the Flipside where I spent so much time.

With Sandros.

"It's not like everything you've been through together has been erased from his memory," Callie says, joining me. I wish she wouldn't come this close to see how much of a wreck I am, how vulnerable, but when her arms slide around my waist from behind, I sink back into her embrace.

High realms, I needed this.

"Will you stay with me tonight?" I ask Callie. "It's just... I don't want to be alone."

"Of course I will. But may I ask—" She turns me gently around to face her. "What are you afraid of?"

"It's not that I'm afraid."

"Come on, Edith." Her voice sounds every bit as healing as I know her hands are. "We've been here for months, and this room has always been your refuge. It's where you always come to be alone, it's your safe place. What has changed?"

My whole body softens as I give up. Callie senses the hurt in people, especially people that spent whole nights with her in the same tent during the war, people with whom she shared adventures in the deadly northern forests of the Winter Realm, and people she survived some seriously dark shit with.

"I'm worried that Durion might get crazy ideas, now that Sandros is here." I walk to the screen that separates the large chateau chamber from the walk-in closet as I speak. It was built centuries later than the room, which makes the place feel like a juxtaposition of two different times, even though the style is in sync. It feels like walking from one century into another.

By the time I reach the closet the dress has slid off my body, and pooled at my feet, allowing me to walk directly into the bath chamber. Callie follows me, taking a seat on the wide edge of the tub as I sink into the foamy water. I let it soak me to my chin like the embrace of a long-lost lover, my eyes closing of their own accord.

"So, you fear that Durion would try to force himself on you?" she asks with the calm of a therapist—I know what those sound like from movies, and find it rather soothing, having someone talk to you like that, with so much understanding, as if nothing you could have ever done could be bad enough to match the atrocities she'd heard from others. Like no darkness were too dark, too inscrutable.

"Not necessarily in the sense that he would rape me, but he might try to force more contact," I explain, enjoying the water with my eyes closed. "He could overstep in the hopes that it would bring about more intimacy between us."

"I can stay here with you. To be honest, your lover Sandros has always given me the chills, and to know he's lurking there, in the forbidden wing... I mean, no offense, I know he's your fated mate and you love him and all, but he gives me the creeps. He has this demon vibe..."

That makes me laugh. "I can't blame you. But the old wing, it's not forbidden, it's just undergoing renovations."

"There are no lights there except candles and torches, and the place is old. The gold-colored stone and smell of old make me think of the dungeons back in the Flipside."

"But there are no ghosts here to wander about. This is the human realm."

"I've heard they have their uncanny stuff, too."

"It's much less common, and nothing we can't handle with all of our experience."

We keep talking until late in the night, and wind up sharing the bed. We fall asleep staring up at the canopy, but in the dead of night the pain that's been pulsing in my chest grows more intense.

I train my focus on the sound of crickets, resisting the urge to establish contact with Sandros' mind. If it weren't for the warmth of Callie as she snores lightly by my side I would toss and turn like a tormented animal. The more I think of him, the more perfect he appears in my mind, the more unattainable. I see myself reaching out to touch him, and him backing away.

It's after midnight, and I'm exhausted from the struggle, yet I can't fall asleep. Sandros Nightfrost is still here, in my head, my heart full of him, that cursed pain pulsing. I run our moments together through my head, especially the memory of our first night together. I lay down in his tent with him, feeling his naked body, basking in his warmth, and the closeness, the intimacy.

Even though he was unconscious, we connected.

I can still feel the electricity that went through my body when our bond was created, the first time we were physical with each other. I remember the dance at the Queen's birthday. The evening I met Durion, too, the only man that ever dared come on to me, which I admired back then. Some others played with the idea of having me, at least for one night. With my telepathic abilities, it was hard *not* to hear their minds, not to see the scenes unfolding in their imagination. But they would have never made a move because I was an ex-convict, I still had a stigma that would never go away.

We had more in common than we knew, Sandros and I. The ladies of the Winter Kingdom lusted after him. Their thoughts were loud as Tartarus, and they often enraged me. I may have told myself they were weak and cheap to secretly drool over a man they openly talked shit about, but deep down I wasn't any better. He didn't have any less of an effect on me.

Ah, what I wouldn't give for one of those sleeping pills that humans take to work for me, too. But sadly, there's nothing in the human realm that can knock me out, not even the strongest drugs. It takes another good two hours until I manage to talk myself down from the spiral of hopeless desire that came with turning this situation on all sides in my head. And just as the weight of my eyelids seems just about there, I feel it.

A presence here with me. Something—or, better yet, some*one*—that shouldn't be here. The finest hairs rise up my arms.

CHAPTER II

Sandros

It's not long until Edith Snowstorm follows my silent call into the forbidden wing of her chateau. I wait for her sprawled in an armchair, running my fingers along the blade of a knife. My suit jacket and my shirt are open. Wearing them all day feels like fucking prison.

I hear her steps down the dusty corridors, and close my eyes for a moment to focus on the sound. Just that—the sound. Every one of those shy ghostly steps brings her closer.

She's enjoyed all this time away from me. She's had her way with Durion Mithriel, she's lived with him openly as his wife. My neck thickens with rage as I imagine her riding him up in the chateau's master bedroom overlooking the misty hills of Auvergne. It's a romantic region this one, almost magical. Most humans dream of visiting France for its enchanting, mythical air. I dreamed of it too, relentlessly, for whole other reasons, reasons that rammed a knife in my back when I spotted Edith at the mayor's party.

I grimace as I remember. What the fuck did I expect, really? I should have seen it coming. There's no changing Edith Snowstorms from a rebel without cause, from a temptress, into a one-man woman.

I've chosen this armchair especially for our meeting tonight. It's large, almost like a throne, with what used to be a white cover thrown over it. It looks like the corpse of a once sumptuous piece of furniture, sumptuous like I thought what we had was. Priceless. Unique.

But as she finally appears in the framework of that archway, the layers of my fury start to fall off like fucking rusty armor plates.

"Sandros," she whispers as my eyes rake over her.

I wish I could still feel resentment. Maybe even hatred. At least the need to hurt her. But all I feel is pain and rage.

She came wearing nothing but the white night gown that seems to flow along her body like a river of snow, her skin glistening like silver in the moonlight. Her hair is white and bluish, as if encrusted with ice, while her eyes are the warmest brown. They're full of sweetness, of longing, of fucking deceit. Because we both know that she's nothing like this image she projects. For a moment I wonder if she even looks like this, if this vision isn't only the product of my imagination that has become morbid and sick after everything this mates' bond has put us through.

I shouldn't have expected her to wait for me. I knew who she really was, I knew her past. Humans have a saying—a snake might shed its skin, but never its ways.

And Edith Snowstorm is a snake. She's a deceiver. This angelic vision of an ice princess once ground her pussy into my mouth with glee. She enjoyed playing my whore, and using me as her toyboy, too. She loved having my cock sunk deep inside of her, and the way she stares at me now, she remembers it as vividly as I do. And yet whoever would set eyes upon her now would swear she's a virginal little angel.

"I thought we had a silent agreement not to be snooping into each other's minds." Her voice is faint, and the rush of blood has stained her cheeks rosy. Some months ago I would have fallen for that look like an idiot.

"I needed to see you. Alone. I couldn't think of a safer way to send a message. I'm sure Durion has you monitored at all times." I examine the knife in my hands as I speak. It's old and rusty, and by the hilt I'd say it's ancient, at least in human terms. "Fascinating object. They must have left it behind when they cleared the museum that this chateau used to house."

"I left Callie in my room. If he goes there—"

"If he goes there he'll think she's you. He won't dare touch her because he won't want you to know he looks in on you."

She stares at me down her nose as if she's just caught me with something.

"And doesn't that surprise you? That he and I aren't sharing a room? If we were together—"

"Edith, don't even," I cut her off. My voice is still low, but thunder builds up at the back of my throat. "Of course you wouldn't share a room while I'm here, in the chateau. Anyway, I got you here because I need your help getting to the Antichrist."

"But if all you need is contact to—"

"I don't know who he is, Edith. You and I, we need to discover his identity first."

She drops on an old cushioned bench with an elaborate back made of wrought iron, dust rising from it as she sits. She blinks rapidly with wide eyes.

"I don't understand."

"I lied to Durion. Nessima never gave this operation over to me, and I don't have the Antichrist's identity. And we have exactly seven days to find out who it is."

"But, but why? I mean." She shakes her head, laughing nervously. "Why would you do that?"

I lean forward, playing the rusty knife in my hands. I must look like a barbarian with my loosened shirt, Edith's winter beauty reflected in my ravenous eyes.

"Nessima didn't send me here. I found my own way out."

"So, she's not *really* your lover?"

If I didn't know better, I'd say there was hope in her tone. But fuck knows I'm not gonna give her that satisfaction.

"I needed to take liberties in order to put my plan into motion. Those liberties were tightly linked with her desires."

Edith's swan throat tightens as she swallows hard. Another scene of her spreading her legs for Durion flashes through my head, and it's all I can do to keep from hurling the armchair against the wall.

"So you did fuck her."

"As you fucked Durion."

"I won't be judged by you," she whispers through clenched teeth.

"No, but if you care about the Winter Realm and your best friend the Queen as much as you say you do, you're going to help me."

She shakes her head. "No, you don't get to set the rules. I need to know your motives, what side you're on, and I need proof that you're not gonna screw us over."

"Listen." I stare at her from under my eyebrows. I give her the next information doing what I avoided to do from the start—establish that connection with her mind that we both know so well, and that we should both avoid. Still, it's the safest way to communicate. The channel is rusty, but enough to pass on the most important information.

"My loyalties lie in the same place they always have—with my brother and my people in the Winter Realm." That she would think even for a second that I would betray them... *"I've got Nessima secured for seven days. My ways are my own. But in these seven days I must find out who the Antichrist is, and stop him."*

Here we are, she and I, sharing secrets again, even though I'd sworn to myself I'd never end up in such a situation with this treacherous siren again. But Edith Snowstorm will remember who her real master is soon enough, and the pleasure of it will fucking hurt.

"I'm going to need more than that, Sandros," comes the reply, her face reflecting the same suspicion and uncertainty as her words that echo inside my head. *"You haven't made it exactly easy for me to trust you. Not only by coming here and selling Durion and me that story so convincingly, but your whole—"*

"My whole history? My origins as a spawn of hell?"

She doesn't need to say it, her eyes say it all. And who can blame her. It's true. Even right now, as we speak, I feel like I'm going to hell. I mean fuck, I wouldn't even trust myself.

"Whether you trust me or not is irrelevant, Edith. You're going to help me."

"And why would I do that? Like I said, you're not exactly—"

"And what choice do you have? Go to Durion, tell him the truth? What would that do for you? Most probably he'll run with the information to Nessima, to secure himself a good position with her and her benefactor once the worlds are under their control. He sucks up to power, you know that. I'm sure you wouldn't put it past him."

She ponders, chewing the inside of her cheek.

"I'm the lesser evil here, and you know it."

"All right, so suppose I go along with it—which is only a possibility at this moment, not a fact—what do you need me for? What would you have me do?"

"All the people that Durion talked about earlier today, you know them. You're in good relations with some of them. You could get me close and, together, we could probe their minds deeply enough."

She shakes her head. "I already tried. All of these people have their own darkness, much more than the average human, so it could basically be anyone. They're all heavy with secrets and sins, but well shielded. Which I expected. Someone of the Antichrist's caliber wouldn't be easily probed." She pauses, weighing the situation her head. I let her, saying nothing, playing the knife in my hands.

"All right, say we manage to identify him or her. What happens then? What are you going to do with the information? And how did you escape Nessima in the first place, and why isn't she searching for you with an army?"

I give her a crooked grin, my eyes fixed on hers. She can never know if she doesn't probe my mind, which she won't in order to make sure I return the favor, and not violate hers, but my face doesn't express half the rage that writhes within me.

"It wasn't easy," I say. "But it was effective. The *How* stays with me."

"All right, fair enough. But I need to know what the plan is *after* we find the benefactor, and what your ultimate goal is?"

"I want to take the power away from Nessima."

"So you want it for yourself."

Her rosy lips tighten as she waits for my reply that doesn't come.

"This is too shady for me. I won't help you."

She stands and turns around, but doesn't manage to take the first step before I grab her arm and turn her around.

"You don't get to walk out on me, not after I've just told you."

"What's the problem?"

I step closer, breathing down her face. "My secret chains you to me, whether you like it or not."

"Well, I don't like it, not one bit."

I stare down my nose at her, assessing. We're now too close for comfort. Her skin no longer emanates winter cool, but heat. Whether it's arousal or infuriation, it's my closeness that does this to her. And things are gonna get yet more uncomfortable. I came here for her, and by the time this is over I'm gonna watch her fall apart under me. I'll watch the awareness spread in her eyes that she'll never belong to anyone but me.

"Listen, you and I want the same thing—the Antichrist's identity. You've been trying to probe these people's minds, but you hit a wall with all of them, because you can't get too deep without being detected, or influenced. Their minds could be dangerous to you. But with me here as your catalyst... Think about it."

"You and me you say?"

"Just like in the good old days."

She tries to yank herself away from me, but I keep her close. She struggles, but I don't move, standing here like a rock with a grip on her arm.

"This might be news to you, Sandros, but the good old days weren't good to me at all," she spits out, sounding more vicious than she ever has. The soft brown of her eyes that used to engulf me like velvet shimmers with frustration in the moonlight.

"I don't think I've ever seen this side of you before." A slow smile spreads across my face. "I think I like it."

"You like what?"

I whirl her around, pushing her across the hall towards the far wall. The room is large, the terrace doors open, the wind sweeping dead leaves inside.

"You standing up for yourself is rather endearing," I growl as I guide her towards the back wall. I'm so triggered I could spit fire. "Or is it your relationship with Poet-Face that you're trying to protect?"

I ready myself for the avalanche of lies she's going to send my way. For her pleas for me to believe that what I saw at the mayor's party, her and Durion kissing, was only a misunderstanding. I steel myself not to punch a hole through the wall when she denies it, but then nothing comes.

She just stares at me defiantly, her lips tight. It is said that the lips show a person's emotional nature, and hers have always been plump, inviting, highly feminine. But it hits me that now they express something very different. They express frustration, hostility. Defense. She's determined to protect herself from me, and probably her lover too. I stifle a laugh, one that would chill her to the bones and remind her who's boss here. But I swear by all the demons, by the time I'm done, she'll remember.

"I see you're not trying to deny it anymore," I say. "Good. We've made some progress—we're honest with each other."

"We're not honest until you tell me what happened with Nessima, and what exactly you're going to do after—and if—you get your hands on her complete power."

"You'll find out at the right time."

"Some things I have to know now. Like, how long after she exiled me did you fuck her?"

"That's your most burning question?"

"It's the only one that concerns me personally."

I say nothing as she talks, spitting out sentences like an angry waterfall. "Her main purpose when she exiled me and kept you was to separate us from each other. She wanted you, not only because you could increase her power, but because she *desired* you. Lusted after you, and she did very little to hide it. And you went on and gave her what she wanted? How long? How long after I was gone, Sandros?" Her eyes fill with betrayal, her lips livid, and fuck knows I can't get enough of the sight.

It does me good and bad at the same time, like delicious nectar that you know will make you sick later. Yeah, let her. Let her imagine me with Nessima just like I've been imagining her with Poet-Face. My own imagination tortured me as I licked my wounds at a hotel outside town. Those scenes still run through my head, and the only thing that soothes me is imagining myself killing fucking Poet-Face right in front of her, and having her watch me gut him.

"How long until you fucked him?"

"I asked you first."

My fingers bite deeper into her flesh as I push her against the cold wall. "Why aren't you trying to deny it anymore?"

"If I do, would you believe me?"

I should just push her aside, and fucking forget it. I should walk away and burn every memory of her and I together. That's what the bigger part of me wants to do, but there's this other part that clings to this moment, to her eyes, to her answer. One that needs to hear it from her lips, and even then it probably wouldn't accept it. A part of me that wants to keep provoking her until she breaks down and tells the truth. But is the truth even what I want?

"You have no right to question me about Durion, and you know what? I have no right to question you about Nessima." She closes her eyes and straightens herself against the wall, her arm muscles relaxing in my hands. "What we had is broken, and I don't think we can save it." She opens her eyes, the curved shield of her lashes rising. And there it is again, the soft brown, treacherous velvet. "That's assuming that you'd even want to save it."

It takes a lot of willpower to resist the urge to drill into her mind. I let go of her arm and slam my hands against the wall, trapping her, my face close to hers.

"Deny it again. Tell me it's not true, tell me there's nothing between you and Durion Mithriel."

"Can you say the same about Nessima?"

I keep it back, all of it. Both the truth and the lies. For a moment she looks older, defeated, the shadow of hurt spreading over her cheeks.

"You dipped your cock into another woman," she whispers, her warm breath touching my face. "And not just any woman, but our biggest enemy. *My* enemy."

"I did what was necessary," I lie.

"Me too." She sticks out her chin, tears shimmering in her eyes as she tries and fails to keep them back. She takes a deep breath as if accepting a hard truth, and pushing herself against the wall, wanting distance from me.

"I'll help you find the Antichrist," she says. "Not because you don't give me a choice, but because you're right—we work better together than we could ever work alone. I need your strength in order to break through the concrete-like defenses of this town's darkest secrets. But once we've gotten them, *if* we do before they get us, that will be that. We're going separate ways."

I let her talk, listening beyond her words. I take in the inflection in her voice, the vibrations. At least about this, she's honest.

"We'll see about that," I rasp, letting my arms drop, but still trapping her against the wall with my body. "You're not exactly free to choose your allegiance. You belong to me."

"A mates' bond isn't a contract. And I've been released from your service a good while back. I don't owe you anything, Sandros."

"No. But I *can* hurt the people you love. And if you force my hand, I will."

"The people I love?"

I stare hard at her, letting her draw her own conclusions.

"You're capable of harming other people, innocent people, just to see me on my knees?"

"There are no innocent people in this game, Edith." I look down from her eyes to her lips to her throat, to her breasts as she breathes. So close, her skin white as alabaster, her body naked under the vaporous folds of her white night gown. "But I wouldn't mind seeing you on your knees. I think you might enjoy it, too."

"You prick," she spits out, trying to leave. I slap my hand against the wall, making her stop. The tip of her nose is very close to my forearm.

"Things can get really dark really quickly between the two of us, Edith," I slur close to her ear. She stands stiffly, not looking at me. I don't think she could look me in the face even if she wanted to. I'm not sure if that's because I disgust her, or because I scare her, but it doesn't matter, as long as she knows there will be consequences if she tries to cross me. I bend closer, touching her cheek with my nose, which causes her to stop breathing. Small beads of sweat appear at her temples, and her scent of winter mingles with the strong scent of woman, telling me that despite everything she still wants me. I still affect her.

"For the record, I don't agree with you," I rumble in her ear. "The mates' bond *is* a contract between us."

"You don't own me, Sandros."

"Oh, but I do." I take my hand off the wall and wrap it gently around the side of her face, my fingers slipping to the back of her head. She's so small in my hand, her alabaster skin glistening against the honey-bronze color of my wrist. I close my eyes for a moment, taking in the feeling. Edith Snowstorm is the only woman that has ever stirred emotions inside me. Trouble is, my emotions are torturous and violent, and I'm not experienced enough to rein them in. Maybe I shouldn't even try. She was mine, and she betrayed me. It's only fair that I take back what's mine, even if this is the only way to do it.

"You gave yourself to another man, but you weren't your own to give." My fingers curl into her hair, filling my palm with it. It's thick, and silky, and warm from the rush of blood through her skin.

"If you can have your way with other people, I sure as hell can, too."

"I did what was necessary, but you—"

"That doesn't mean anything," she bursts out, but lowers her tone immediately, probably for fear we might get caught. My cheek twitches. She must be more scared that I'll rip Poet-Face's head off if he walks in on us, rather than that he would do anything to harm me. "I want you to tell me how it happened, I need to know. I have the right to know, because your relationship with Nessima has many more implications for the worlds than what I might have with Durion."

My throat muscles tighten as another flash of her and Durion punches into my brain. I pull her hair, causing her to hiss and squeeze her eyes shut.

"The nerve on you to say that to me," I grit out. "What's your excuse for letting that asshole's hands all over you?" I tug at her nightgown, trying hard to stop in time and not tear it off of her. "Do you go to him like this often? Do you push it off your shoulders, slowly, watching his cock rising?" I pull her hair to tip her face up to me and, in an impulse I can't suppress, I crush her lips under mine, a rock hard demand on juicy plump flesh. It's a violent kiss, meant to remind her that I'm her bane.

She moans into my mouth. I'm not sure whether it's protest or encouragement, but the scent of her hormones can't be lying—she's surprised as fuck, but in a good way. Her heart jumps in her chest, I can feel it as I press my own chest against her, pushing her against the wall and basking in the feel of her body on mine. My hand grapples for the lower part of her dress, lifting it feverishly, seeking her flesh. I find it and run my hand up her thigh, my cock rising.

I release her mouth to allow her to breathe, and give myself a respite, or I will do something that I'll regret. The thought of being inside her again has been the driving force behind each and every one of my decisions lately, it was the thought of her that fueled me to do everything I've done.

I thought she felt the same. And yet I found her in the arms of another man.

"Stop, Sandros, don't do this."

"No, you're right. I shouldn't even want to do it." I cup her face and tip her head back, her white-blonde hair forming a halo on the dark wall. "I shouldn't even want to look at you after what you did."

"Stop saying that," she counters through her teeth. "You're not an innocent. I'm not the only traitor here."

Yes, you fucking are, I want to blurt out, but I hold back.

"I should forget that you fucking exist. But this fucking bond won't let me relinquish what's mine."

"You're doing it because you can't bear the thought that you lost a possession. An asset. This isn't even really about me."

I push my cock into her mound. She flinches at the rocky hardness even through the gown gathered between us.

"Still think I'm confusing you with an asset?"

"You know what I mean." She manages breathlessly, but the scent of her hormones is going wild in the air.

"Our bond isn't an asset only to me, but to you as well, Edith. Together, we can discover who the Antichrist is. Maybe we can even defeat him."

"Or her."

I nod, and let her go slowly. I'm even slower to step away from her. Her eyes fall to my hand as I grab my cock, trying to rein in my erection. My shaft is twitching, and I'm gonna get blue balls soon, but despite this need to take her right here against the wall, I regret what I just did. It scared her, I can tell by the way she breathes, and now she's petrified. Even if it messed with her hormones, it also hit the wrong buttons, not to mention what it's doing to me.

"I suppose I have no choice but to work with you on this one," she manages, but it clearly costs her effort to pull herself together. She takes her hand to her lips clearly on an impulse. "You're right that we stand a better chance together. But I'm going to need you to promise me something."

"Promise you what?"

"It's more of a pact, actually."

My laughter echoes through the abandoned grand hall of the forbidden wing.

"Hush, someone will hear." She makes to move over to me, but then she stops midway. Of course, she was afraid I would rape her just a few moments ago. If it weren't for her scent that betrayed her arousal, pain would punch into my chest now, thinking that my touch made her feel dirty, that her heart recoiled from me and filled with guilt because she'd betrayed Durion against her will. But even though I might be an asshole for what I did, at least now I know she still wants me.

And she'll never want anyone the same way. She's fighting herself, trying hard to resist me, but I'll break her defenses and have her on her knees, where she belongs, sucking my cock. Soon, I would have my sweet revenge for her betrayal even though alone wanting that makes me fucking weak.

"After we find him, we defeat him. Or her. Together. It won't be easy, but it's a must. You won't keep that power for yourself. If you want to try and take over the Winter Realm, it will have to be by other means. You can use Nessima's minions or whatever, you can stay with her if that's what you want. I don't give a damn if you want to marry her, but I won't let you have the Antichrist's power. And when this is over, know that we'll be on different sides, which will probably make us enemies."

"Sounds like a good pact. But why are you so sure I won't cross you once I have what I want?"

She juts out her chin with a special kind of confidence that I see for the first time. "Because when this is over, I will drill deep into your mind, and stay there."

"That would be like prison for you."

"It will be worth it. It's the only way to ensure the safety of my friends and my home. But tell me this one thing, Sandros. Why? Why would you try to take over the Winter Realm? How did you become infected with Nessima's ambitions, you, the most loyal soldier of your world?"

"You'll find out one day. Once you're trapped inside my mind, there will be no escape from the truth anyway. Maybe you'll realize that it's not as bad as you thought, or that it's worse." I step away from her as I speak, back into the far recesses of the hall, away from the moonlight. Darkness swallows me, but she can still see my eyes glowing from the shadow like a wolf's.

I stop here, holding her gaze as she stands in the beams of moonlight.

"The goal doesn't excuse the means. So whatever your ultimate purpose is, it doesn't justify *this*."

"In love and war, everything is permitted."

"And what is it between us? Love or war?" She whispers.

The shadow closes, swallowing me completely.

CHAPTER III

Edith

A tremor of pleasure runs through me as I lay eyes on Sandros. He's just arrived, and Durion is introducing him to the mayor and Giancarlo as our distant cousin. Everybody's jaws have dropped, even though some control themselves better than others. Thankfully, I'm one of them. I've had a good teacher at masking my emotions, namely Sandros himself, and I've learned that lesson well. Unfortunately, I didn't learn all of his best lessons. If I had been a really good student, I'd now be able to steel myself to hate him for the way he treated me.

Instead here I am, wetting my panties just by looking at him, which shouldn't even be possible. How can a man hold such power over a woman? If all mates' bonds feel like this for the female, then the high realms played a nasty trick on us, because I can't imagine the cauldrons of Tartarus can be any worse than this.

Nobody notices, but my fingers tighten around the stem of the glass of sparkling wine that I'm holding. I can't help but glance at the mirrored wall to my side, hoping that I look my best, even though I shouldn't care. I'm wearing an emerald green wrap dress that stays true to the shape of my body, the lower part like a tight cone on my legs down to a bit under my knees. The stilettos enhance the elegant look, making me seem almost queenly. My hair is up in a not-very-elaborate bun, a few wavy strands hanging loosely here and there, but they're shiny, and white-blond, which to the human eye looks like jewelry. I'm also wearing emerald earrings, but they are small, meant to frame my face a certain way rather than impress, unlike the dangling diamonds of other women here.

I think about how Sandros likes ethereal elegance on a woman, and I'm beginning to suspect that, subconsciously, I've groomed myself into his ideal type. I'm weaker than I thought. I should know better than to even want to look good for him. He was ready to take me against my will only days ago, and it wouldn't have been a demonstration of love, but one of domination.

And yet pleasure runs through me every time I remember how he claimed my lips, no matter how unromantic that was for him. To think that he believes I betrayed him, and that he could replace me with any woman here if he wanted to makes me scratch the back of my head like some sort of psycho woman. I mean look at him in that shiny Brioni suit. Every woman here is 'checking him out', as humans call it, some more overtly than others. Well, all the women except Simone Carrera, Antoine's fiancée and the rich heiress that plays the centerpiece of this fancy party. If there were ever a perfect image of the 'strong independent woman', it would be her. She stands in the middle of the room with a glass in her hand that she sips from as rarely as I sip from mine, deep in conversation with Count Guerin and a few other guests of note, all men. Her fiancé Antoine is nowhere to be seen. In fact, I don't think I've seen him at all tonight.

What surprised me from the moment I saw Simone wasn't only how pretty she was, but also how she is by far the most interesting woman here. There's an intelligent spark in her very dark eyes, she wears a natural make-up, and looking at her laugh lines is enough to give one a jolly feeling. She's got enticing lips, even though you can tell she's a smoker—even though she mentioned she recently quit in the short introductory conversation we had earlier, but she's still struggling with the cravings. There's something of a twenties' diva in the way she wears her hair. She's a refined woman, like a French feminist writer, but she's also got a fresh vibe about her. I like her, and I think the feeling is mutual, even though I haven't probed too far.

My eyes don't rest on Simone as long as hers on me, but return to Sandros. His chiseled beauty ensures that he glows among nobles and intellectuals as much as he does among soldiers and thugs, and his power of intimidation is everything I remember it to be. He makes everyone around him either cower away, or seek his approval to the point where it's embarrassing.

We lock eyes for only a moment. I give him a slight nod—we're ready. He's going to help me direct my energy through the attendees and catch on the one with the darkest streak. For that, I need to find a quiet place where I have an overview of everyone at the party, but also privacy. I need to stay out of everyone's sight, which isn't easy with the looks of a fae, especially when you have fashion designer Giancarlo Botini hunting for the opportunity to talk to you.

"I just met your husband's distant cousin," he says as he finally gets me. "He's quite something, I must admit."

He leans his chin over my shoulder, the ice clinking in his whiskey glass. I can't believe he's wearing his signature sunglasses even on a Saturday night at a fancy function at the Michelin-star tower restaurant on top of the hill, but I suppose there's no taming those inferiority complexes. The more I see of Giancarlo the better I understand how come he hasn't found success yet as a fashion designer, and still depends on other people's finances, his only true power being his ability to charm those people.

I wonder if I could start my probing of the town's most prominent folk with him. He's open to me, and I might be able to do this without much of Sandros' help—the high realms know how I want to delay that moment when the two of us will have to connect again. I wouldn't be able to resist him. I want him too badly, which means that the only way to keep the ounce of dignity I have left is to stay away from him.

Only that our mission won't allow that for long.

"He is," I say in a sweet voice. "Quite a magnetic personality."

"Have you known him for long?"

"Almost as long as I've known Durion."

"Makes sense. I mean, Durion is as handsome as an elf from those Lord of the Rings movies, but Sandros—" He sips his drink, sunglasses in the direction of Sandros. "He's a real-life Greek god. Everything you imagine Zeus would be. Or maybe Hades. No woman in her right mind would choose to be with Durion after having met him first."

"They are both extremely attractive men." I sip my champagne, and release a lie that I desperately need to believe. "I don't compare them."

"As you are an extremely attractive woman." His sunglasses turn to me, his lips glistening in that specific way that only fresh hyaluronic acid and lip-gloss can achieve. "If I didn't know better, I'd think you're members of the same family. Or the same sect." His suspicion and subliminal message doesn't fail to reach me.

"We're friends, aren't we, Edith." He wraps an arm around my shoulder. "You know you can tell me anything, no matter how crazy."

I extend my feelers, carefully and gently reaching for his thoughts. Good grief, he believes Durion and I are siblings that are sleeping with each other. I mean, we do look a lot alike, and not only because we belong to the same 'species', but because of our hair, our skin, and even our eyes, but still. Our features aren't similar. Seems that Giancarlo Botini is even more perverse than I thought.

"I will share some of my crazy with you, if you share some of yours in return." I lower my voice to the specific frequency that I know will melt his defenses. His arm tightens around me with unwelcome but necessary confidence.

"How about we talk in a more intimate place." He lets his shielded gaze wander up the cone-like walls of the tower with their countless galleries and nooks.

With a half-smile, I follow him up the stairs, making up strategies in my mind to get rid of him if he gets handsy.

The nooks are carved in the medieval tower walls, adorned with low orange lighting that reminds me of torch flames and secret love affairs. As we climb the stairs towards the nooks, I look down at the crowded restaurant, searching for Sandros. As large and intimidating as he is, he should stand out from the crowd. But I can't see him. With my channels now opening wider like budding flowers I can hear the fashion designer's thoughts louder. His fantasy goes wild as he imagines what he'd do with me in that nook.

"Tell me," he says as he holds a chair for me at a round cozy table by the arch that offers a view of the restaurant downstairs. It's an almost comical view, with people swarming around like ants in fancy clothes. "Why do I get the feeling that Sandros Nightfrost is part of your crazy?"

"You're perceptive." I breathe evenly, readying myself to dive into his mind, and expecting to find all kinds of perversions in there, but not never-before-seen perversions. In my line of work, I've grown difficult to surprise. Still, I have to go about this carefully, because he's highly sexually charged. He's thinking about fucking me even as he pours me a glass of the expensive champagne he believes I like.

"The truth is he and I had an affair behind Durion's back." There. This should shock him out of his sick horniness. "But I don't know what's worse—the fact that I did it, or that I can't bring myself to regret it." I know I've already got Giancarlo. He likes all talk about sex, drugs and violence, and I'm throwing nuggets at him. That will open the darkest corners of his mind up to me.

"How did it happen?"

I give him a version of Sandros and me doing at an expensive function in the South of France, then in a small unsupervised room in a museum. Scenarios that he likes. I let my true feelings for Sandros show as I talk about him, my guilty desire for him shining through. I hope this sharing of secrets will make Giancarlo feel we are kindred spirits.

Giancarlo is damaged in the head, but most humans are, just like the fae, and if there is a way to get to the deeper part of him, this is it. I keep leading the conversation to where I feel his darkness flow and, finally, there it is. When the lights dim in order to plunge the restaurant in the semi-shade necessary for a great French diva to take the stage downstairs, he uses the chance to bend forward.

When the diva's voice rises and the lights fall, Giancarlo lowers his sunglasses, allowing me to see his eyes for the first time. My breath catches.

"You gave me some of your crazy in exchange for some of mine. I'll give you more than just that. I'll give you a secret. One that can make your most forbidden dreams come true. There's a devil among us, Edith." He speaks so low that his voice is almost a ghost's whisper. His pupils are so small they've almost vanished completely, swallowed by wide disks of very pale blue. If I didn't know better, I'd say the man was possessed, but as he lets his thoughts run free I catch a glimpse of the truth. He's not who Sandros and I are looking for.

"He promised me my most burning wish. For that, I paid with the light of my eyes—and yet I can see." He grins. "As I can see your beauty, shining from the inside. You're not human, Edith Snowstorm. You don't have to hide that from me because I *see* what's out there. It's a gift that came to me in stride. A gift from *him*."

I swallow hard. This isn't the Antichrist, but it feels like he's related to him, like some sort of minion.

"What do you *think* I am?" I tread lightly.

"Maybe an angel? If there are demons, then there must angels out there, too."

"Oh, there are demons all right. But I haven't met the one you're talking about."

"I figured. You seemed oblivious, that's why I mentioned it. Even though I must admit, at first, I thought that you came here to hunt him down. That you were sent to save us from eternal damnation." He laughs coyly as if at his own adorableness, which makes my mouth twist. "By us I mean those who, you know, made a deal with him."

"He made deals with more of you?"

"Just with the needy ones in town, I suppose." He closes his eyes, sparing me the sight of those hair-raising irises for a moment while he sniffs me like an animal. "Your skin even smells like his. As if you were made of the same mold, only that one of you is good, and the other is bad. Hell, you're probably not even made of clay, like us mortals. What *are* you made of? No, don't answer that, I don't need to know, it doesn't matter. What matters is that you can help me."

"Help you?"

"Help me break this deal with him." Something lights up in his eyes as he says that. Like this is where he wanted to lead the conversation all along. He licks his enhanced lips, making me think of a drooling mollusk-like animal running its tongue over its mouth.

"That could be an option," I lie opportunistically, my muscles so tight they hurt. "But for that you would have to tell me who we're talking about." I lean forward. "Who is the demon, Giancarlo?"

He gives me another one of his smiles he believes are so damn adorable. "Aren't you curious to know what my wish was? What I sold my soul to the devil for? Because if we *are* going to make a deal, you and I, *you* would have to provide what *he* promised me."

I tilt my head to the side, feeling my way carefully around his motives. "You doubt that he'll deliver on his promise?"

"What I doubt is that my eyes will be the only price he'll want from me." He stops before he spills too much information.

"I understand," I muse. "And what is the wish that I would have to make come true in his stead?"

"Success. Fame. Applause. This whole fashion design thing, it's a cutthroat game. It's not enough to have an Italian name, and design cute clothes. Unless you hit it real big real fast, you can't survive. It's eat, or be eaten. The competition is fierce, status is a must. So, I needed financial and PR help. In short, I needed a miracle."

"And that's when *he* came into your life?" I imbue the 'he' with the influence that should get him to give me a name, but it's not enough to sway Giancarlo.

"Yes."

"Who is he, Giancarlo?"

His gives me a flashy grin. "I'm not done telling you about my wishes and desires. Before I move from one protector to another—"

"But you already said—"

"Yes, but that's not all. There's something else that I want from you, something only *you* can give me."

"Success, fame, those are already big prizes." I bend forward, letting my senses feel deeper into his mind, my own entertaining the possibility of helping him get those things. I'm sure I can work something out with a witch or wizard in the Flipside, or even ask Sandros to call in the many favors he's got lined up from the higher realms as well as the Underworld.

But then I sense the evil spreading out through Giancarlo just like it did through Eldan's system when he attacked the Queen. It's the same kind of power. Giancarlo Botini is a possessed man, but not in the sense that humans understand possession. He's a servant of the bigger power that is the Antichrist, and yet what he tells me now is his own will.

"I want a night of pleasure with you, Edith." He licks his lips as his pale blue eyes measure me up in a way that makes my skin crawl.

"You can't be serious." I say through my teeth. "To all the women here you're the hot-shot designer. You can have any woman you want, models, noblewomen, you name it." I look demonstratively down at the restaurant, everybody raving to the diva's tunes.

"None like you, and you know it." He leans closer over the table, and I'm pretty sure that if I were looking at him, he'd risk plunging in for a kiss. I keep my attention on the restaurant, but my nostrils flare from the nastiness that he radiates. "You're an angel. How many opportunities does a mere mortal get to bang a fucking angel?"

"Or I could bash your head in and get the information out of you." Both Giancarlo and I sit up, our heads snapping in the direction of the voice.

Sandros walks into our small loge-like nook, hands pushed into the pockets of his pants. His suit jacket hugs his powerfully shaped body over a white shirt that contrasts with his honey-golden skin in that way that never fails to make my mouth water. Nothing in his face shows it, but anger is blazing off of him.

I stand in his way before he reacts on impulse, putting a hand on his chest. His pecs bulge through the white shirt, pumped with the energy of destruction.

"I'm sure Giancarlo is going to be reasonable about this," I say pacifyingly.

I look back at the fashion designer, hoping that he'll back down, but the evil aura has closed around him completely, intensifying his perverted desires that he wouldn't be able to shake even if he wanted to. He leans back in his chair, shielding his eyes behind his sunglasses again.

"You're in lust with each other big time, aren't you?" he says. "You make a sexy couple, I have to say. But wait—you're not actually a couple. Because you, Edith, are with Durion." He sucks on his lower lip, his overly whitened teeth showing. "Isn't lust one of the seven deadly sins?"

Sandros takes a step forward, his chest hard as stone under my hand. He stares daggers at Giancarlo.

"Two angels, falling prey to lust," Giancarlo continues, making me wonder about his mental sanity. Sandros radiates menace, and his sheer size could crush Giancarlo.

"Who says that I'm an angel?"

Giancarlo measures Sandros from behind the blackness of his glasses, pursing his pumped lips. Something about him reminds me of a snake.

Snake.

The word anchors itself in my head. The Serpent is the devil's symbol, and it's particularly powerful here in the human realm.

"Don't," I whisper as I sense Sandros' lust to grab Giancarlo. "We'll need more than just a name from him, so hurting him won't help." I pause. I don't like having to say this. "There's more than the demon we're looking for. He's got...minions. Giancarlo is under the entity's control."

Sandros' face changes as he looks at me and, for just a moment there, I think he's at a loss. Only a moment later I realize it might not be because of Giancarlo, and my heart somersaults.

"Ahh, the passion between the two of you." Giancarlo grabs his cock through his pants. Disgust runs through me, but I can't show it, or Sandros is going to go off like a bomb. "It's safe to day that I'm moved. So much so that I want to watch the two of you getting it on before I stick my own cock in you, Edith."

"Or I sew that dirty mouth of yours shut," Sandros hisses. "Right after I knock all of your teeth out."

Giancarlo laughs. "We both know you're not gonna do that. You need me to be able to use my mouth for more than just lick your girl's pussy. You need me to tell you what you want to know."

"We'll find another way to get what we want." As Sandros reaches inside of his jacket pocket, I catch the glint of a dagger. It would take him a split second to slit this poor bastard's throat open. A mixture of pity and alarm drives me to place my hand gently on Sandros' wrist.

"It's not worth it. Just let him be."

"Ah, for fuck's sakes, even angels should know good business when they see it," Giancarlo says, the snake inside anesthetizing him against the anxiety that any sentient human being would feel at being surrounded by Sandros' killer energy. "I can give you the name you're after, and the rest of the people that name controls. All you'd have to do in exchange is something you both would love, too."

"You can go fuck yourself—"

"Names, Lord Sandros." Giancarlo holds up his fingers. "Multiple names."

"I need just one."

"The hands that he uses to do his dirty work are as important to his game as his own person is."

Sandros looks at me, raising an eyebrow questioningly.

"I, I don't know what to say," I stammer.

"Come on, you know you want it as badly as he does." Giancarlo licks his lips, his hand moving down to his pants again. I look away.

"This can't be happening to us," I whisper. Sandros lifts my head gently with two fingers so that I look up into his golden eyes.

"Just say the word, and I'll slit his throat for you," he says, loud enough that Giancarlo can hear him.

"We need that name."

"Not for this price."

"The whole world is at stake. We don't have that much time anymore."

His jaw tenses. "So, you're saying you'd sacrifice yourself for the greater good."

"Yes." I square my shoulders, and lie. "For the greater good."

But it's only a matter of time until the walls I built around my innermost desires will come tumbling down in front of him, and he'll discover just how much of a fraud I am. How glad I am, deep inside, that I'll get to feel him again, no matter the circumstances. I'm thirsty for him like someone who's been in the desert for days. My eyes move down his neck to his golden chest, licking my lips as I imagine slipping his buttons out of their holes and stripping him. It would feel like unwrapping a gift. But then a flash of him fucking Nessima hits me. In my vision, Nessima replaces me in the forbidden wing of the castle where he got me the other night. Bitterness hits my tongue.

"What is it?" he whispers huskily.

"I just can't forget that you've dipped your dick into another woman."

"I don't like being kept waiting," Giancarlo interrupts. From my peripheral vision I can see his hand moving in his pants, and my mouth twists. "Get on with the show."

"You expect us to do it here?" Sandros snaps.

"What's wrong with that? I mean, I know it's close to public sex, with the risk of being caught and all, but look." He motions down to the full restaurant downstairs. "Everybody is absorbed by the diva's show. No one can catch you. Besides, they're down there, at your feet." A grin stretches under his sunglasses, making him resemble an ugly alien. "And you like having people at your feet, don't you, Sandros Nightfrost?"

"What makes you say that?"

"I don't know, just this feeling I have when I look at you. Somehow, I can't believe you're an angel. No, you can't be one. You're a demon, aren't you? Like *him*."

The truth of it crawls up my spine.

"So, if I were to guess, I'd say you like your women on their knees in front of you, writhing with desire and clawing at your pants to take your cock into their mouths."

The thought of Sandros and Nessima punches a pain into the pit of my stomach, making me wonder how I'm any different from a masochistic teenager. I look at him again, handsome and unattainable and cool as the winds of the Winter Realm as he gives Giancarlo the death stare.

I curl my fingers around his wrist.

"Don't, please. He's not fully in control of himself."

"We'll find another way to the Antichrist," Sandros declares.

"Come on, do it, demon boy," Giancarlo grunts, his face red with arousal. "You know you want it. Consider me the audience you've always wanted to have. Don't try to deny it. You've been wanting to brand her as yours. To show the world that she belongs to you, so no one would dare come too close. You might not be doing it for love, but whatever there is in that black soul of yours wants to suck her down and consume her, and it might be even more powerful than love."

If the snake has more insight into my bonded mate's mind than I do, I should be seriously worried. Instead, it sends pleasure up my spine. I know whatever feelings Sandros might have for me are far from the sweetness and selflessness of love, and yet the poison of Giancarlo's words is intoxicatingly gratifying.

Unable to say what I want, I decide to just act on it. With an almost crippling fear of rejection, I slip a finger between two buttons of Sandros' shirt. It stuns him. He doesn't even move as my fingers work, slowly, my fingertips sporadically brushing his skin. He doesn't even look at my face, but down at my hands, his attention yet focused on Giancarlo. When my hands slip under the sides of Sandros' shirt, ready to peel it off of him, Giancarlo loses control. He gets up, radiating the intention to join us.

Sandros inhales through his teeth, his large hands wrapping around my wrists and pushing them down. Before I know it, he's already over Giancarlo, throwing him down and breaking the chair in the process, then pins him to the floor with a knee on his chest.

"What the hell," Giancarlo shrieks, looking stricken. The sunglasses have flown off of his face, the pale blue discs he has for eyes filled with confusion.

"Yes, hell," Sandros hisses. "Hell is where you'll be going, paying off your debt to your Antichrist, if you don't give us what we want. Here. Now."

Giancarlo tries to grin, clawing on to some of his confidence, but Sandros pushes his knee harder down into his sternum. The man's ribcage cracks under the pressure, my stomach knotting at the sound.

"Sandros, please," I try. I've witnessed Sandros' violence before, in the war, but a human's suffering is disturbing. They're so much weaker than us fae. Yet Giancarlo is a possessed man.

His thoughts and feelings reach me, since he's unable to keep the lid down on them any longer, betraying secrets that I probably wouldn't have reached under normal circumstances. I hate to admit that maybe violence *is* the answer this time.

"Give us the name," Sandros repeats.

"Guerin," the designer blurts out. "Count Guerin is seeing him soon. He's the next to strike a deal with the Antichrist. We've been after him for a long time."

"So he's using you to get access to the town's finest," Sandros growls.

"Guerin has a lot to gain from a deal with him, too."

"I don't give a fuck about the old shark's motivations. I'm interested in the Antichrist. The name." He presses harder, this time also grabbing

Giancarlo's jaw and pushing his head against the floor, just as the diva's extraordinary voice rises in an enchanting mix with the back-up vocals, finishing her performance in a grand style.

"All right, all right," Giancarlo screams, everything that held him together unraveling. Tormented by pain, he's completely at Sandros' mercy.

Finally, we are on the brink of a breakthrough. Within seconds, we're going to learn the name of the man we're up against. But when Giancarlo opens his mouth to say it, nothing comes out. He tries to push out the sound, both Sandros and I can see that. He struggles, his throat thickening, but soon he panics.

"Get off him, Sandros, you're cutting off his windpipe."

Sandros jumps to his feet, but even with the burden lifted, Giancarlo coughs like he's about to spit out his lungs. He gets on all fours, retching, his eyes protruding, his neck thick and reddening.

"We have to help him." I want to throw myself down and do it, but Sandros catches me.

"Don't. The evil is still inside him. I don't want you too close. It could be looking for a new host."

I claw onto Sandros' shirt, pushing my face into his chest, unable to watch Giancarlo's demise. There are things you don't get used to even in war, and watching someone die in pain is one of them.

"And this is only the beginning," Sandros says, now connected with me, and reading my mind.

I'm deeply grateful for the connection, and he must know it. It's like a pillar that I can hold on to, knowing that I can never fall as long as he's in here with me.

"We're not going to get the name out of anyone," Sandros concludes as Giancarlo's body softens, the life draining out of him and leaving him limp on the floor.

"The moment they make a deal with the Antichrist, he leaves a piece of himself inside them," I complete Sandros' train of thought. "That piece strangles them from the inside out before they can betray him."

"Our only lead then is Guerin. We'll have to follow him at all times. We can't blow this. It might be our only chance."

My eyes stick to Giancarlo's body, but I become increasingly aware of the crowd downstairs in the restaurant. "What do we do about his body? Should we call the police? They're going to start an investigation sooner or later anyway."

"Better later than sooner. I know this will sound heartless, and it will hurt your sensibilities, but we don't have time for the fuss the humans will make around this. We've got a monster to catch. Probably the greatest monster of all time."

"And yet nothing seems bigger to me than the loss of life, be it human or supernatural." Worry engulfs my heart. "I'm worried about his soul, too."

Sandros ponders for a few moments, and connected as I am to him, I know he's searching for a way to put my mind at ease. "I have an idea."

CHAPTER IV

Edith

Sandros buried Giancarlo's body in the thickest part of our garden at the chateau, right behind the forbidden wing. The forbidden wing is also where we are now, in the same hall where he lured me a few nights ago.

"I should go," I whisper, rubbing my arms and turning to leave.

"Wait." He stops me in my tracks.

"I have to get back to the main wing before Durion realizes that I'm missing."

"Durion won't be back for another few hours, I had Callie make sure of that. Plus, your heart is still aching for Giancarlo." He stops behind me. Even though I'm not facing him, I can feel him towering over me, and I forget how to breathe. He smells of manliness and the shadows of the underworld.

"He's buried behind the well that I used as a portal," he says. "When this is over, we'll get his body to the Winter Realm, or the Flipside, and find a mage or a high priest to help us save his soul." He wraps his big, warm palms around my upper arms, giving me a kind of comfort that messes with my head. "I know that's what you want."

I also wanted to suck your dick in front of Giancarlo. I squeeze my eyes shut, straining to keep this part of my mind closed to him. Sandros has always thought the worst of me, for the most part because he chose to, but now I'm starting to think that maybe he's right. How much of a wanton must I be to fantasize about having his cock down my throat publicly?

"Thank you," I manage. "But now if you'll excuse me, I'm exhausted. And the thing with Durion, well, better safe than sorry."

"Are you actually *eager* to get back to him?" He starts massaging my shoulders, slowly, forcing my body to give into his touch while my mind rebels against his scrutiny. Damn it, I need to resist him, eve if it kills me.

"Let us set one thing straight, Sandros. You lost me when you slept with Nessima. Don't act now like I belong to you, because I have no intention of being one more fool in your harem."

"You will be whatever I please, because you *do* belong to me."

I can't believe this outrageous bastard. But I won't be getting anywhere with him if I fight and accuse, I've learned that much.

"Tell me something, Sandros. It would have been so easy for you to find out the truth about Durion and me, if you really wanted to, if only you looked deeper into my mind. Why didn't you do it?"

"That would have been violating your privacy."

"Oh, so it was morals that stopped you. How about not violating my body, then?"

"I may be a thug, but I'd never cross that line with you. You must know that. Besides, it's not your body that I'm interested in conquering." He bends down, his lips brushing my ear. "It's your will."

His warm breath mists the shell of my ear, his big hands moving down my back, and wrapping around my waist. I don't stand a damn chance. I can't resist leaning back into him, my head resting against his chest, my eyes closed.

"What about Nessima?" I strain myself.

"Is that relevant right now?"

"Always." I take a deep breath, because I want this, but I'm scared of it might reveal, too. "I need to know."

He doesn't protest as I sink into his mind, his memories closing like water above my face. I see Nessima sauntering over to him in high heels, pushing her black dress off her shoulders, staring into his eyes. It's in that room at the estate where we've all been together one last time before she exiled Durion, Callie and me to the mortal world and kept Sandros to herself.

Anguish closes a fist around my heart the closer she comes, and I can't watch anymore. I pull back before she even stands in front of him.

"I can't do this." I jolt to tear myself away from him. He doesn't let me.

"Keep going. Keep looking," he says.

"I can't."

"I insist."

"It's hurting me."

I start a pointless struggle in his arms. His hands are firm as Tartarus as one wraps around my waist, and the other one around my neck. He presses me against him, and his erection pushes into my buttocks, heat traveling up to my face with the speed of light.

"Look deeper. Watch what happened."

"I'm not in the mood for porn, thank you, especially not the kind that involves my fated mate and his mistress."

"Oh, I'd say you're very much in the mood for porn." His nostrils flare against my cheek. Of course, all he needs to do is smell me to know exactly how I'm feeling. He knows my frustration, the hurt, the lust, and there's no damn fooling him. "The kind that involves you and your bonded mate."

"What about Durion?"

He turns to stone, only his breath still waning and waxing on my cheek. I stiffen like a rabbit in the claws of a panther. He smells the truth off my skin. But while his body remains motionless, his other senses crawl all over me. He enters my mind, slithering along the lining that leads to my story with Durion. Everything seems to play backwards in my mind, now reflected in his, all the way to the night Nessima exiled Durion, Callie and me from the Winter Realm.

He runs through every day and every night that Durion and I spent in each other's presence. He also remembers the first time he came into the mortal world, went looking for me, and found me in Durion's arms, almost kissing at the mayor's party.

I let him go as deep as he needs to, my body softening into his arms. By the time he's done, I'm no longer sustaining my own weight, abandoned to his embrace. But the first words that come out of his mouth are not what I expected.

"You kissed him that night."

"It wasn't for real Sandros, you know that now."

"It had happened before, that's what I know. He'd used every chance he got to make demonstrations like that. You didn't respond, but you didn't exactly turn him away either."

"Why do you insist on seeing me in the worst light possible?" I try to turn around and face him, but he keeps me pinned in this position. "You refuse to see reason, you—"

"I refuse to give in to my self-deluding tendencies."

"What?"

"You think I don't want to believe I'm the only man you ever wanted?" His hand moves down my neck to my chest, slowly, his touch a caress and a threat at the same time. "Of course I do. You have no idea how often I found myself making excuses for you. Telling myself that you had no way around it, that, if you'd had a choice, you would have never chosen to be with him, that he forced your hand, that you were doing it for some ulterior reason I couldn't yet fathom."

"And that is all true."

"What's also true is that his hands have been on you."

"I never let him touch me this way, Sandros."

"Maybe not, but you had his lips on your skin, and you didn't pull back."

"You know damn well—"

"Here is the only thing *you* need to know," he slurs, kissing my cheek gently with those sculptured lips. It sends the blood rushing through my veins as if it were happening for the first time. "Things are going to change now." He plants soft kisses down my neck as he speaks, his hand slowly lifting the lower part of my dress, while the other one sinks into my hair, giving me sensations that make me question my sanity. This is a man stating his power over me, not his love, so what am I doing, getting wet for him?

"You were once placed at my disposal, as my servant. When the war was over, you got back most of your liberties. But you were never really free from me. We already shared a bond, and when that connection turned into a lovers' bond, you became—" He kisses my shoulder as his hand moves under my skirt, grazing the inside of my thigh. "My slave."

I let loose a sigh, leaning my head back against him. I can't help moving my body into his touch, wanting him to do it, to slip his fingers under my panties and touch me there, touch the most private part of my body. But he's intention is to torture me, not to pleasure me.

"You are still mine, Edith. Many things in your life might change, but that won't, no matter how many battles you win."

No. I will always lose the war, as I'm losing now against his fingers that fist into my hair and tug, his lips finding their way to my collarbone. I'm like play dough in his hands, at the mercy of his lips, craving them to close over mine.

I turn my head to the side, lips half parted, inviting him to do it. My heart beats fast as his mouth closes over mine, hot and carnal, the warmth of his body wrapping around me along with his familiar, masculine scent. It's a symphony of fragrances, Sandros and rain on the air as he leads me backwards, his lips subduing mine. When I hit the wall he grabs me under my thighs and lifts me up so that I have to take him between my legs.

"Sandros..."

"You want me to stop?" He's kissing my neck as he says it, going downward.

"That's what I should want," I whisper, my fingers sinking into his hair, wanting to keep him there, but he's got other plans. He interlaces his fingers with mine, pinning my hands against the wall. The look in those golden eyes sends guilty thrills down my spine.

"But what *do* you want?"

"I want you to take me again. Take me like the first time we did it." I don't get to finish the sentence that he covers my mouth with his. His lips mold mine slowly, his tongue enticing me to open my lips and let it in.

It's a deep, sensual kiss, a mix between lust and power, his hands keeping mine against the wall. Those hands travel down my arms, caressing my body on their way down to my legs, and slipping under my dress again. His fingers brush over my silk panties, and my skin prickles in anticipation.

I moan, leaning into our kiss, wanting more of him.

"What man wouldn't worship your body," he rasps, staring down at my body like it's some kind of magic. It sends butterflies from my stomach all through me. "Those bastards at the Winter Court, those who stigmatized you and talked behind your back, they would do anything to be in my place."

Just like the women would do anything to be in mine, but my breath is way too erratic for me to talk.

"And Durion, well." He runs his tongue over his teeth, dealing with an aggressive impulse. "I suppose he saw an opportunity and seized it. But you—"

"Don't," I cut in. "Don't say I didn't do enough to keep him at bay."

He grabs my hair. This time, it hurts a little.

"Look deeper into my memory. Watch what happened with Nessima."

"I don't want to. It would hurt too badly."

"Do it. It's an order."

"You're no one to give me orders, not anymore."

"Oh yes, I am, and you damn well know it." He pushes me downward, the stare of a master on his face.

"Do it," he commands as he guides me downward to my knees. As he does that, he forces me took into his memory, too.

I'm back in that scene where she was walking toward him.

She stopped in front of him. My mouth dries as I see her bottomless dark eyes hanging on his. Even in their demonic opaque blackness her feelings dance like flames. There's hope in them, and the desire to be seductive for him. To be everything *I* was, or at least for him to see her that way.

Only that it's not Sandros who's looking at her, or at least not the *real* Sandros. This person is somehow...clad in his image. I squeeze my eyebrows as I go deeper into the creature's identity, snapping right out of this memory when I recognize him. It's Killian, Nessima's number one servant, the entity she created to do her dirtiest work.

"What in the world? What was *that*?"

"Killian doesn't have a will of his own," Sandros explains. "He was created as a vessel for Nessima's will. As the humans like to say, I hijacked that will. Now he's carrying mine, and Nessima doesn't have a clue. A glamour spell gave him my appearance in her eyes, but it won't hold up for much longer. Hence the seven days we have to find the Antichrist."

"So Nessima thinks you're still there? And the one she's actually sleeping with is Killian?"

"Yes."

I manage little more than to mumble as I try to wrap my head around this. A chill runs down my spine as I imagine Nessima riding the monster she created, thinking it's the man of her dreams. I have a flash of her reveling in the creature's arms, and a wave of pity hits me. Then I remember she didn't pity me for one moment, and she would have done way worse to me than she did if it hadn't been for Sandros. "But how? You need magic in order to do that."

"The people serving Nessima, not all of them are in a powerless trance. They don't have magic of their own anymore, because she took it away from them, but they're connected. They pointed me in the right direction."

"So, you're basically leading a revolt against her?"

"Let's just say I knew how to pick my allies, and then got under their skin."

"By the high realms," I breathe. "That must have been one hell of an operation."

"It wasn't easy to put it together. But the thought of getting you back kept me going." He tugs again at my hair, enough to punish me with some pain. "I was alone among hundreds of enemies. Only the idea of you in my arms again kept me going. I risked my life every fucking second at the Blackfall estate only to come here and find you in Poet-Face's arms."

He undoes his pants as he speaks, keeping my face close to it. As magnetic as his eyes are, I can't help lowering mine to the erection he just whipped out of his pants. I'm here, on my knees, with his veined and purple-headed cock right at my lips. I lick them in guilty anticipation, and when he pushes his engorged cock through them, I moan, offering zero resistance. I open until my jaw hurts, trying to take him all in.

He groans as he fills my mouth, the sound mingling with my muffled moans. I've been trying to put myself off Sandros, quit him like a drug, yet here I am, giving in to his poison. I can't resist my impulses and reach between his legs, cupping his balls through his pants. His upper lip curls over his teeth as he inhales sharply. I stare up at him as I shamelessly suck him off, kneading his balls and wanting to feel them on my tongue. I hook my fingers into the waistband of his pants, pulling them down, my fingers brushing ropey hips. I squirm against the wetness between my thighs as my fingers splay over his muscular buttocks, my mouth sliding down his cock. My neck swells and my face burns from his sheer size, but there's no stopping me.

Sandros thrusts into my mouth, unbridled. Yes, that's it, fuck my mouth, is what I'd tell him if my mouth weren't full. My jaw hurts, but there's a violence to my own lust that won't let me stop even if he wanted to. I keep him with my hands splayed over his buttocks, feeling them flex. He pulls my hair tighter as his cock engorges inside my mouth, his warm seed hitting the back of my throat.

"No," he groans as he empties himself into my mouth, my tongue and my cheeks closing greedily around him.

This is what I wanted. This is me stating my power over him, but I can tell he won't let me have it for long. He won't indulge in the pleasure, even though I'd love to keep watching it on his face. As expected, my delight is short-lived. He scoops me up and pushes me against the wall, throwing his suit jacket off, and putting my hands on his chest, under the sides of his shirt.

"Take it off. Do it like you want me so fucking much it hurts." He's ready to ravage me. "Come on."

The aftershocks of his own orgasm are still coursing through him, and yet he's so much in control it's frustrating. I take off his shirt, my knees trembling, soreness still pulsing through my jaw.

"It's not that I don't enjoy having you on your knees, and running my cock down your throat. Hell knows I do." He leads me away from the wall and into the moonlight, where he turns me around and locks an arm around my waist from behind. We're looking into a mirror that's more of an old gothic relic with a silver frame, our faces glowing in it, milky white next to golden honey.

"It's what I wanted," he rumbles in my ear. "You remembering that you've always been mine, and that my power over you hasn't ended with the war. But you don't get to do what you want with me, when you want it, Edith. You don't get to watch me fall apart." His hand slips under my dress and into my panties, so slowly and deliciously that it's torture. "I'm not your toy boy. I'm your master."

He curls two thick fingers into my already soaked pussy. My back stiffens and my hand locks around his wrist, traying to get some control over the sensations he's giving me, but it doesn't help. He drives his fingers deeper, doing things to me that only he knows how to do.

"This is mine and only mine," he says in my ear. He watches my reactions in the mirror, biting his lip as my eyelids flutter and my cheeks flush.

He rips the upper part of my dress off of me, his fingers tangling with the rags as he reaches for my breasts, covering them with one huge hand. My hips move against his fingers as I rise to the balls of my feet, moving to meet the pleasure he's building up inside me. He could get me there so easily, yet he tortures me, playing with me, letting me chase it like a cat chases a dot of light. Heat courses through my body, blood rushing to my cheeks as I reach behind my back and grab his cock over his pants. He didn't button up before, so I can reach in and grab him over his briefs.

I find him as hard and hot as he was in my mouth, and it gives me pause. Did he stay hard all along?

"Ah, what you do to me," he rumbles, his chest vibrating against my back. His large hand still covers both of my breasts, my dress a ripped mess tangled between his fingers. We're all milky-white and honey skin, all sweat and hormones, my back molding his godlike body.

I reach into his briefs and wrap my hand around his cock, moving slowly but tightly up and down his length. It needs wetness, and my senses go into overdrive. I rise on the tips of my toes, but my dress is still in the way.

"Rip it off of me, Sandros," I pant, sweating and wanting. "I want us naked."

"No."

"Why not?"

"If you want it, beg for it."

"Please."

"Not ask. Beg."

"I beg of you."

A delicious groan comes from his chest, sending a tingling pleasure over my skin.

"I want you more than I have ever wanted any woman in all my centuries," he says in my ear. The more he conquers my senses, the more connected I am to his mind and heart. "Which is also why you must understand that you can't even look at another man. Ever. And we have centuries ahead of us, Edith. You and me, the bond we have, you can see it as your own personal prison."

He curls his fingers sensuously inside me, dangerously close to my sweet spot. I gasp, grabbing on to his wrist with one hand, the other around his cock. It throbs in my hand, demanding that I start giving him the pleasure that my touch promises. His blood runs hot through his veins, I can feel it, and I want nothing more than to break him, make him give in again.

"No, my sweet," he says, reading my mind. "You did that with me just once. Now, your lust and your pleasure are mine to control."

"I can't bear this anymore," I say breathlessly, letting go of his wrist to reach down and lift my own dress. Before he can react I bend forward as much as his hold will allow, and guide his cock to my pussy, his fingers still inside me. "Please, put it in. Just a little bit, please."

"That's my girl," he slurs, easing his fingers out of me and grabbing my hair. He bends me over, his reflection in the mirror rising over mine like a god made of honey and bronze, his body glistening, his long hair framing that chiseled face. He looks wild, and powerful, and unbreakable, and yet the hunger in his golden eyes hints at his vulnerability.

Sandros Nightfrost has a soft spot for me, and knowing that gives me the greatest high. Satisfaction fills me along with his cock as he enters me, my soaked walls parting ravenously to take him in.

"High realms! Yeah, Sandros, fuck me."

He moves slowly at first, but his grip on my hair betrays how much he wants to thrust, and how much control it costs him not to do it. I watch him in the mirror, wanting to see him come undone for me.

And the only way I can get that is by giving in.

I chase the pleasure. My thighs quiver as I gyrate on his cock, my arousal feeding off the sound of him making way through the slick of my wetness, the smell of sex filling the air. As I grow comfortable with his size I slam myself backwards into him, skin slapping skin, my breasts bouncing.

Sandros licks his lips, eyes on my tits, big hands clamped on my hips. But it's my face that's going to make him come, and I know that. I don't even try to hold back my orgasm because I won't be able to anyway, so I give him what he wants. I grip the sides of the mirror as my pleasure explodes around him, my mouth open, my eyes squeezed shut, my cheeks burning.

"Ah, fuck, woman," he grits out as his cock starts pulsing inside me, releasing waves of warmth into my womb.

It's long moments of lingering pleasure for the both of us until we come down from our high, and our eyes meet in the mirror. We both know it.

Tonight, something changed forever.

Edith

SANDROS AND I WALK quietly into my room, but inside ourselves there's a clamor of thoughts and feelings.

We didn't take precautions the first time we did it either. We'd found ourselves in a situation between life and death, but we should have thought about the possibility of pregnancy. Just as we should have thought about it tonight. But that's the problem with the passion between bonded mates. No danger can keep you apart, and pregnancy tends to be one of the main focus points of such bonds. So it's no surprise this happened. But the two of us, we have the weight of the world on our shoulders, as well as a mission that could get us both killed, and we're a very unlikely pair. Our bond came to be under unusual circumstances, and having babies never crossed our minds. Now that this is happening, we're both stunned.

"Edith, I—" he begins in a low, caressing voice, but I stop him with a finger on his lips.

"We can't talk about this now. We have bigger fish to fry. The Antichrist..." The words catch in my throat. I don't have to say it to the end. Sandros knows better than anyone what's at stake here for the world. And for him.

"We don't have much time left with Nessima either," I whisper, leaning my forehead against his bare chest. I should preserve the distance between us, but what I do instead is splay fingers over his pecs under the sides of his shirt. I breathe in his scent. He still smells of us.

"What happened between us, it—"

"It will have consequences, and it's not just about the seed I planted inside you," he finishes for me, and kisses the top of my head. It's one of the few tender gestures he's ever made towards me, but it's deeply felt. His body tenses as he decides to step away, but whatever it is that we have is that compelling. I can see he fights himself, but he loses the battle and wraps his arms around me, his big hands tangling in my hair almost lovingly.

He presses those carnal lips to my cheeks, and only now I realize that I'm crying. He kisses away my tears, but when he rests his forehead against mine, I see his jaw clenching. Something about this upsets him.

"I'm sorry for this bond between us, Edith. It's my fault that it came to be. If having my baby in your womb makes you cry, then it is clear to me you never wanted this connection. It has been forced on you, and I fucking hate it."

His words hurt. My throat is full of tears, but my lips stay locked. I can't express what I feel. I never knew how deep and intense a mates' bond could become. We're so melted into each other it's hard to draw the line. But one thing I know for sure—he means every word he says now.

"But I can't imagine any other man ever laying a hand on you, so when we were together, tangled in that moment, that pleasure so close to bursting, I just... I did it on purpose, Edith. I'm sorry."

I wish I could say something, but all I do is swallow the tears in my throat, trying to keep them behind closed lids. But my defenses are flimsy, and easily torn when Sandros tilts up my head, his golden eyes arresting mine. There's no resisting him when he kisses me. I melt into him with a muffled moan, running my hands under his open shirt, enjoying his skin on my palms. Enjoying knowing that he wants me, and that he would even get me pregnant to ensure that I stay his.

He cups my head with his large hand, keeping me in place as his tongue pushes its way between my lips, claiming my mouth in long, lustful strokes. He leads me to the bed and lays me down on it, prowling over me on his hands. My legs open easily, allowing him to position himself between them.

"Since we're going to hell, right?" He smiles at me, and I pause at the sight.

"What is it?" he asks, his voice a velvety caress. It's the strangest thing, hearing tenderness in his rumbling, deep tone.

"I don't think I've ever seen you smile before. Not like this."

"It might be the last chance I get."

His words feel like a rock weighing heavy on my chest.

"We're headed nowhere good, Edith." He covers the sides of my face with his big warm hands. "The world might fall apart soon, and I might have to go down with it." Our connection is deep enough now that I understand what he means, and the rock gets heavier. "But I promise you, no matter what happens, if the Antichrist hurls the whole hell at us, I will protect you. I will make sure that you and—" He glances down at my belly, surely feeling as strange about the word as I do. "—you and the baby are safe."

I can feel his hard knuckles against my pussy as he works his pants to free his erection, lifting the remains of my dress quickly to put himself in. He wraps his hand around my jaw as he enters me, slowly, his width opening me up as he looks down with me.

"Watch," he commands gruffly. I look down at his big bronze cock as he pumps into me, my own juice glistening on him. I arch my hips to meet his moves, grinding into his pumping, our sweaty thighs grinding against each other. It's a wistful dance, Sandros rising on his knees to push himself deeper inside me, and me grabbing to the sheets, and arching up in both pleasure and pain.

I move faster against to meet the roll of his hips, his cock filling me deep and wide, the slick sound and smell of our union filling the air.

"Say that you'll forgive me," he says, his big chest heaving as he's close to coming. "Even though I can't bring myself to regret what I've done. I put my seed in you to mark you as mine no matter what happens. So that no one else can have you even after I'm dead." He growls deeply as he comes, furrowing his brows and baring his teeth. I love looking at him become the beast, because I know it's the most real side of him.

I watch him release himself inside of me, and I swear I could cum just from that. But he plays my clit with his thumb just the right way, because he instinctively knows what I like. He covers my mouth with his hand as I come undone for him, screaming his name, the sound muffled against his big hand.

He comes down over me, covering my mouth with his when a new sound joins our heavy breathing. The sound of clapping hands rips through the air. Sandros moves as smoothly as a snake when he rises to his knees and zips up, buttoning up his shirt and shielding me from the visitor's eyes in the process. He makes sure that I've gotten to cover myself with the bed sheets before he jumps to his feet and faces the intruder.

Except I know who it is before he even steps into the moonlight.

Durion.

"Quite a show, I must say." He tries to keep a mocking face, but his cheek is twitching in that way it always does when he's frustrated, angry, and often poisonous. I get off the bed and step next to Sandros, finding shelter under his arm, even though I know he would prefer me to stay back on the bed where he can keep me behind him.

"Even though I do find it quite disrespectful of you, Lord Nightfrost, to come here and have sex with my woman in my own house."

"I'm not your woman," I bite out, pushing myself into Sandros' side, his powerful arm tightening around me.

"I know everything, Durion," he says. "She was never yours. You can drop the charade."

"I might not need the charade anymore, but I do still have leverage," Durion grunts, grabbing a slender woman's arm from the shadow and pulling her forward. It's Callie, her already big eyes even bigger from both worry and embarrassment. She looks like she doesn't know exactly what she's doing here.

"You are going to need a healer if you're gonna go against the Antichrist," he continues. "And she's not gonna be here, because she's leaving with me, going back through the portal to Nessima. I'm sure she won't be happy to know that you've been screwing your old mate girl Edith behind her back."

Sandros' jaw clenches as his eyes shoot daggers at Durion. The possibility of him running back to Nessima and telling on us has been hanging over us like a malevolent shadow this entire time, and we both knew this would happen if we stopped being careful. But what chance did we stand to resist with everything that's been boiling between us?

"You don't have a portal," Sandros counters.

"You will give me yours, because otherwise..." He squeezes Callie hard enough to make her yelp, and it makes me to want to jump at him, but Sandros holds me back.

"We've got the Antichrist to deal with—"

"You lied, Sandros," Durion interrupts angrily, shaking Callie, hurting her. High realms, I want to hurt him so badly. "You don't know who the Antichrist is. You're not here because Nessima sent you. You're here for *her*." He points a shaking finger at me.

"As if you didn't know that from the start," Sandros says through his teeth.

"Well now you're gonna pay the price," Durion cries. I've never seen him like this. Spittle flies out of his mouth, his face is red, and his soft brown eyes with the curved lashes seem to be changing into something almost grotesque. "You're gonna give me the portal," he calls, squeezing Callie's arm so hard that she cries out, her body twisting. "You're gonna—"

But before he can say it Sandros is already over there. He grabs Durion's hair and kicks his shins from behind, causing him to fall to his butt with a thud, humiliating him on purpose in front of Callie and me.

"Listen to me carefully, you piece of shit," Sandros says close to Durion's face, his upper lip curling over his teeth with every word. "I came here with only one purpose—getting the Antichrist. As for Edith, what she and I share is something that neither of us asked for, but that neither of us can turn away from. Trust me, we both tried, really hard. So we will be together for as long as we can, and nobody is going to stand our way, do you get that?"

"Let me go," Durion manages, his voice thick, but Sandros doesn't care. His fist clenches, his big knuckles showing, getting ready to send a punch Durion right in the face when the latter manages to save himself in a desperate attempt to speak. "I can help you! I have new information!"

Sandros' fist stops an inch from his face.

"Guerin," Durion hurries breathlessly, taking his chance. "He's been found dead tonight. Fell right out of a closet at his house, he was buck naked, and there was a pentagram on his back."

I can feel the blood leave my body, right into the ground.

"No, it can't be," I cry. "He was our only chance to get to the Antichrist in time."

"The last person he was seen with was Simone, his son's fiancée. I already made an appointment with her tomorrow evening, she'll be expecting us."

Silence falls over the room. Sandros' face is frozen, his golden eyes fixed right between Durion's eyebrows like poisoned arrows. If looks could kill, Durion would now be lying in a pool of his own blood. Lucky him that we still need him.

CHAPTER V

Sandros

After centuries of doing what I do, you can smell war on the air. And now, as I'm looking up at Count Guerin's chateau from the driveway, the smell of death and foul intent hangs around me like the clinging evening mist. The count's chateau is very different from the one that Edith, Durion and Callie occupy. It looks more like a bastion, or a fortress with high round walls and crenels. It almost feels like home—dark, gloomy, ancient. And even if it's not ghosts and ghouls that we'll find inside, the attendees of this meeting are no less sinister.

Simone Carrera is the first person to greet us with a glass of champagne in her hand. She signals the butler as soon as she sets eyes on Edith.

"Bring the lady one too." She turns to Edith with a wide smile. "I opened an insanely expensive bottle. I noticed that you love champagne as much as I do. The liquor of the gods, am I right?"

Edith answers with a smile, but there's a slight strain on her forehead, a tension in her cheeks. She's probing Simone, who motions to the cushioned sofas for us to sit down. Edith takes the invitation, but I prefer to stand next to her, while Durion and Callie both take a seat.

"May I offer you something to drink, Lord Nightfrost?" Simone says. "Durion tells me you like—"

"When and where was the last time you saw Lord Guerin?"

Simone's eyebrows shoot up. It's obvious she's not used to being interrupted. This woman is used to power and position, and she's sure as fuck not used to coarse bastards such as me, or at least she doesn't usually have to take their shit. I can sense through Edith that's what she's thinking right now.

"I didn't realize you were an investigator, and this was an interrogatory."

"I'm sorry, we don't mean to be brusque or crude," Edith says sweetly, but I'm all for brusque and crude, so I cut in.

"You just don't seem very affected by your loss. Your future father-in-law died just yesterday, and yet here you are—" I give her a once-over to make a point, "—having champagne in a red silk night robe like it's date night."

"I see you're not familiar with the relationships between this family and me. I don't owe you an explanation either, but I'm going to make an exception, since we have an exceptional situation."

She walks around as she speaks, the red silk robe waving behind her as she motions with her glass of champagne to the portraits that adorn the wall.

"The count's family. Father, grandfathers, great-grandfathers. No women, as you notice. As if they brought themselves into the world. As if it was their pussies that tore to pieces while birthing a human being." She stops to glance at me, communicating her meaning. Oh, that's right, she's a feminist. Here in the mortal world women have to fight for equal standing among men, which is very different from the order of things in the supernatural realms. Equality is a given there, the hierarchies and oppressions take place on other levels. "You see, Count Guerin and I came together for the sake of business. The marriage between Antoine and me wasn't even a done deal yet. Well, almost done, but still." She raises her arms like a surrendering diva wrapped in silk and champagne. "So here it is, the truth. I didn't like him. He was a misogynistic bastard like his son and all men that came before him in this family. So yes, I do not give a shit that he's dead. I do care who did it though, because there's obviously a murderer among us, and any one of us could be next. I understand Giancarlo Botini has gone missing, too."

"Do you happen to know if your father-in-law was seeing someone after he saw you?" Edith asks, her tone much sweeter and accommodating than mine. When Simone looks at Edith, the look in her eyes changes. It's not only softer, but also less combative. Admiring? There's a feeling that appears on her face along with her smile and the laugh lines that make her charming in a masculine kind of way.

"He wasn't my father-in-law yet."

"But you'd known each other a while, so you must know who he was close to," Edith inquires carefully.

"I was getting there," is all the woman offers.

"No offense, you seem unnaturally calm and comfortable considering what happened," Durion puts in.

"Is that why we're here?" Simone says. "To accuse me of Guerin's murder? Come on, give it to me straight."

"Listen, Miss Carrera." I step forward, closing the space between us at a slow pace. "I hate to agree with Lord Durion, but Count Guerin died an extremely suspicious and a violent death, and yes, we do have a good guess who it might have been. It's why we're here, and why we asked the police to help us arrange this meeting with Lord Guerin's most private circle that attended last night. The police agreed to help us with this—" because I bribed them, "—and it will look bad for you if you refuse to cooperate. I imagine you don't want to become their number one suspect."

Simone chews on her lower lip, her eyes traveling over all of the attendees. Edith, Callie, Durion, her butler. She nods at him, and the man starts immediately to the main door.

I don't back away as we wait, towering over the woman, too close for her comfort, but she still manages to hold my stare in a way that few people ever could, even supernaturals. There's a strength about her that sets her apart, and makes her my number one suspect. She hates me being in her private sphere like this, but I need to smell the darkness on her. Because she does have darkness, and she also has secrets, but I'm not sure whether there's evil in there, too.

What I do realize quickly is that I have none of the effects on her that I'm used to having on women.

She's neither impressed by my unusual looks, nor is she flustered by my proximity. I think she's intimidated by my size and my stony face. She thinks I'm unpredictable and dangerous, but I have a feeling she knows I would never hurt a woman, and that she's safe. I get all that through my connection with Edith.

"How do you put up with him?" she addresses Edith, stepping away from me and heading over to her. I raise an eyebrow, watching her approach my bonded mate like a guy would. "He's sexy as sin, but such a cocky bastard."

"I don't understand." Edith straightens her back, her eyes raised up at Simone who stops in front of her without sitting down. There's something masculine about the way she does that too, as if she doesn't even belong in her skin.

"Come on. If we're gonna uncover secrets here tonight anyway, why not start with yours? You and Lord Durion say you're together, but ever since Lord Nightfrost here made his entrance, you haven't been able to take your eyes off of him. Everybody noticed the way you look at him."

Few things have made me hold my breath all through my centuries of life, and this is all of them.

"You're in love with him," Simone concludes, measuring me up and down with...is it envy? "I don't blame you, but men like that, they never change, you know."

"I don't know what you mean," Edith says, squaring her shoulders. She keeps cool, like the experienced spy she has become throughout our time at war, and it makes me uncomfortable. If she's able to fake her feelings with Simone, is she able to fake them with me? No, it can't be, since we share this telepathic bond, yet something tells me I'll never stop being insecure about her. But I put a baby in her belly. I've secured my place in her life. We share something that will bind us even beyond the connection we already have.

"He's a man made and bred for war," Simone says. "He will always be battling something, in some form. He can't live any differently, and he can't give you the warm and fuzzy kind of love you desire."

"I can give her protection," I say through my teeth.

She smiles her wide smile where the laugh lines become so obvious. "So you admit it. You're having an affair, the two of you."

Since the cat is out of the bag. "It's more than an affair."

"Is it?" Edith's eyes hang on mine as if there's nothing left of the world except the two of us.

"Hello, I'm still here," Durion grunts, his eyes blazing with frustration, his narrow cheeks red.

"Oh, I'm sorry, Lord Durion, I didn't mean to disrespect you," Simone says. "It's just, since your own woman doesn't seem to take you seriously, I figured why should I?"

"I would be very careful about offending me, Miss Carrera." Durion says bitterly.

"Oh, there's actually a pair of balls in your pants?" I chime in. "Easier to hang them out when you're confronting a lady, is it?"

I can't wait for the bastard to do something stupid with all the tension he's accumulated, but just as I'm getting my hopes up, the butler walks in with the rest of tonight's attendees.

"Madame Simone, Monsieur Le Mair and the twins are here," the man announces with a slight nod and a polite gesture of his hand.

Jean Dubois appears behind him, belly first, angry face following.

"Monsieur Le Mair, thank you for coming," Simone greets him.

"If this is a joke, it's a very bad one, Madame Carrera," the mayor huffs, swiping a glare over us from under knitted bushy eyebrows. He radiates anger, but as I follow Edith's telepathic lead, it reveals itself as anger that stems from pain. It's almost touching. He was in love with Giancarlo. The man's disappearance has him panicky, but he can't afford to show it, since he's still not 'out of the closet', as the humans say.

Edith and I feel deeper into him, tapping into this darkness, but at the moment we find only the repression and secret that choke his soul, twisting and partly mutilating it. As for the twins...

"Why are the children here?" Edith asks the inspector that accompanies Jean Dubois, her eyes filled with concern. "They weren't supposed—"

"They were there last night, too, madame," the inspector replies. He locks his hands behind his back and takes a place in the corner, next to the butler, which will allow him to observe the room the whole time. "Lord Sandros said that everyone related to the victims' closest circle should come, no exceptions."

The twins keep close to their father, holding hands and staring ahead of them, seemingly at

Durion. He stares back like an angry older kid getting ready to bully them. And when I thought this guy couldn't sink any lower.

"Inspector, this is absurd," Simone protests. "They couldn't possibly have anything to do—"

"Lord Sandros asked specifically that they join us as well."

"They can't be suspects," Simone insists, looking over at Edith for support. But Edith is now silent. Through our connection, she understands why I did it. There's darkness surrounding the children as well, a special kind of aura that's imbued with the same hellish energy that everyone here seems to carry.

We must get the Antichrist here, today. Problem is, he or she wouldn't let themselves get caught so easily. So, if they're here, it's because they wanted to be, and Edith and I know it. It's also what we counted on.

Whoever the Antichrist is, they are going to be here tonight, if everyone we requested comes.

Edith and I need each other to identify the person quickly, but what she doesn't know is that, right after we do, I'm gonna get her out of here—and that's what Callie is here for.

Antoine de Auvergne, son of the dead Count Guerin and supposed fiancé of Simone Carrera is the last to make his entrance. He's late on purpose, of course. It's one of the few things where he can still do to exert control over others, because otherwise he's nothing but a sad old drunk, and he's not even thirty yet. His fiancée gives him an especially contemptuous look. I narrow my eyes, wondering why she wanted to marry him in the first place. She's a resourceful woman, desired among the noble and the rich, definitely has a bunch of much worthier suitors, not to mention that she's not even into men, so what's the catch here?

Antoine is drunk, as always, precariously cradling a bottle of whiskey in his hand and failing to find balance on his feet.

"So what is this circus?" he stutters, dropping onto the sofa too close to Edith. She moves gracefully a little farther, probably sensing the danger mounting in my body. I'm this close to fisting his shirt and hurtling him across the room.

Simone's eyes fly to me, saying everything her mouth isn't saying. If her relaxation around the old count's death is suspicious, how about his own son's?

"I'm sure we don't have to remind you that your father suffered a most terrible death last night, Lord Antoine," the inspector says in a chaffing tone. "He fell dead from a closet, with a pentagram carved onto his back. He was still warm and bleeding when they found him."

Antoine bends forward with his elbows on his knees, his head down.

"And just as my friend here had managed to numb me a little." He shakes the bottle in his hand to make a point. "Thanks, I guess I needed the reminder."

Edith and I take a sample of his inner turmoil. There's powerless frustration inside, the most frequent reason why people drink in the human realm, but he's so intoxicated it's hard to tell genuine feeling from alcohol-induced sadness, chronic depression and existential angst. He's what the humans like to call a 'hot mess'. I suppose he would be just the right kind of candidate for the Antichrist to possess and manipulate as he did with Giancarlo, and yet Antoine doesn't give off the same vibe. He's a human in decay, but still, he is his own master. Also, I don't pick up on any sense of purpose or desire in life, and these people are insanely difficult to lure.

I look at Edith. The hellish powers in here are thickening, which means the Antichrist is among us. This is the part where tension mounts, and we get to work—probably the most dangerous kind of work we've ever done. For all we know, the Antichrist could be manipulating everyone here like they did Giancarlo, they could have them all dead within minutes, or have them attack us with malevolent powers.

So we steel ourselves to do what we planned. We nod at each other, so slightly that only the two of us and Callie notice. Callie's hands tighten over Edith's. She's the only one that knows my entire plan—she's supposed to get Edith out of here as soon as we've identified the bastard.

"So why are we here, inspector?" Antoine manages. "And why are *they* here?" He motions to us.

"Consider us security," I say, folding my arms across my chest.

"I already told the police everything they wanted to know," Antoine says.

"So have I," Simone puts in, and drains her glass of champagne.

"I just wish you'd actually start with the investigation already," the mayor blurts out, stomping over to the liquor table and completely ignoring his children. "Whoever did this to Guerin is gonna go after one of us next."

"No they won't," I say. "Because whoever did it is here now, and we're gonna expose them."

Silence falls over the room. The inspector furrows his eyebrows and unclasps his hands form behind his back, staring at us intently. "Where are you headed with this, Lord Nightfrost?"

"Inspector, if you care to use the money that you've received for this little arrangement, I suggest you leave us now," I say evenly as I take off my suit jacket and start rolling up my sleeves. "You might want to take the butler with you, we won't be needing his services anymore."

"Wait a minute, what the hell do you think you're doing?" Simone reacts. "You don't get to send my staff away."

"I'm ensuring that what's about to happen causes as little collateral damage as possible," I reply, unfazed by the woman's outraged tone. I walk over to the cold fireplace from where I can face the room, resting my hand against the mantlepiece. If I'm going to do this, I'm going to need the power of fire instead of ice, of hell instead of my homeland, and this fireplace sure comes in handy.

"I'm sorry, Lord Nightfrost," the inspector counters, reproach lurking in his tone. "I helped you with this because you asked me to and, well, I thought, a man of your standing—"

"My social standing didn't interest you, Inspector, it was my financial means that did."

"However," the man continues after a moment of awkwardness. "This is still my investigation, and whatever is going to be revealed tonight, I want to be here, and hear it."

"You'll regret it, Inspector," I say dryly.

"Possibly."

"Surely."

The butler steps forward and takes a bow, his eyes darting to everybody in the room one last time. There's fear in his eyes, as if he feels something in the air. "If Madame approves, and I'm not a suspect, I would like to take my leave."

"Go," I respond instead of Simone, which earns me an indignant gasp from her. The butler seems to care about as much as I do, because he throws off his white gloves and scurries out the door like this is his one and only chance to escape a haunted house before its walls crush him in. Unlike him, the inspector steps closer, folding his arms over his wide chest, eyebrows furrowed. I continue according to plan, but I stay aware of Edith every single second, ready to protect her at all times.

"You will find it hard to believe," I begin, "but one thing we know for sure—Count Guerin hasn't been killed by natural forces."

The first reaction comes from Antoine.

"What are you saying, that Satanists carved that pentagram into my father's back? That's ridiculous. Whoever did it sure wanted to make it look that way, I won't say no to that, but I really don't think it was them."

"I'm not saying it was Satanists or anyone trying to make things look like they did it. I'm saying it was supernatural forces. I'm saying it was Satan. Or better yet, his offspring."

Dead silence follows, the wind howling outside like a bad omen. This time it's the inspector that speaks up.

"So... You mean this is the Antichrist's work?"

A shiver goes through Edith, I see it from the corner of my eye. I just hold the inspector's stare, watching his eyebrows unfurl and rise to his receding hairline. The corner of his mouth trembles before he starts to laugh, but that laughter is insecure and it quickly fades. As he looks around himself, he realizes most of the others aren't as shocked by my statement. The twins stare him dead in the eye out of their ice-blue irises, still hand in hand, Simone plays with the now empty glass of champagne in her hand, looking down at it with puckered lips as if avoiding the inspector's questioning look, and the mayor sits down slowly in a chair with a face that says 'Finally it's out there.' Only Antoine seems stricken.

"Aren't you people going to say anything?" he blurts out, springing to his feet in outrage. He loses his balance, but catches himself quickly against the back of the sofa. "This is absurd. Is this why you got us all here, why you're poking at my fresh wound?"

"Oh, come on, Antoine, just drop it," Simone cuts him off. "You didn't give a shit about your father. If anything, you've been waiting for this moment for years."

"I didn't want him dead, you pussy-eating bitch!"

Something close to bloodlust flashes in Simone's face. She's ready to fling her glass at him, and maybe I should let her. The dark energy in her already builds up, but that may be because he exposed her sexuality in front of everyone. But then I sense Edith through our connection, nudging me. She's got something here.

"Why did you want to marry him if you're not even into men?" she asks quietly, almost like a hypnotist. "I understand that you didn't *need* what Count Guerin had to offer, so why sacrifice yourself like that?"

The woman doesn't reply, but keeps staring at Antoine with murder in her eyes, her lips tight. She's bubbling up, and maybe we should make her spill.

"Why don't you tell us about the last time you saw Guerin?"

Her dark vibes whirl around her like growing thunderclouds. The tension is so thick that the inspector feels compelled to reply in her place.

"She told us they were discussing the terms of their arrangement right after the diva's performance. It was in the rooms behind the restaurant. It was just the two of them and no witnesses. She wanted to back out of the arrangement, but he insisted he could give her something she wanted, and no one else could give it to her."

"He was blackmailing me," Simone finally blurts out.

"Was it about your inclinations?" the mayor wants to know, a spark of hopefulness in his eyes. I watch the expanding exchange form behind narrowed eyes. The mayor seems so absorbed with this whole thing, that he's completely oblivious to his own children. I'm beginning to understand the scope of emotional neglect the twins have been subjected to. The fact that their own existence has served to make this man look good in society has left an ugly print on their auras, too.

We originally planned to let the Antichrist make the first move, but we might as well attack first. It would give us more advantage than to let him or her pick the moment.

I raise my hands, close my eyes, and summon my own hellish power. The doors rattle for a moment, then bang shut, causing the inspector to jump and turn around, not knowing what hit him.

As my eyelids lift to reveal my irises again, the room fills with gasps. I can feel the glow in my eyes, molten gold and heat.

"What the hell is happening here?" Antoine stutters.

It's been centuries since I've tapped into my mother's legacy, and I'd hoped I'd never have to do it again. But it takes great power to fight something as mighty as the Antichrist, and the power of my mother, Lilith, is one resourceful pit, however murky and filled with horror.

Yet this horror might take over me. I've dealt with a lot of fucked up stuff in my life, but this is a whole new level of evil.

It whirls harder above our heads as the Antichrist prepares to reveal himself, probably sensing there's something bigger afoot here than they expected. Demonic power increases its flow through my veins, helping me feel for the foe. Their energy recoils from mine at first, realizing that I've tapped into something that will strip them of the veil that covers their identity soon. But now that I've hooked my claws into the powers I've inherited from hell, it's time to get my bonded mate out of here.

I haven't used the demon power of my mother in centuries, but it's like riding a dragon. You never forget how to do it. Whenever you climb up again, it's like you never dismounted. When I spin around and hurl flames into the fireplace, it's as the last time I did it was only yesterday. They catch on the logs and surge, sending gasps and ripples through the room.

"What the fuck," the inspector yelps, while Antoine forgets all about his intoxication and leaps to get Jean Dubois' children out of the way. His instinct surprises me.

I turn around, feeling my way through the emotions in the room, still with Edith's help.

"Come on, let's go," Callie cries, trying to drag Edith after her, but my bonded mate pulls back.

"There's not a chance in hell I'm leaving him alone in this," she says, loud enough for the entire room to hear her.

"You must," Callie insists desperately.

"Yes," I command, my voice changing. "You must leave, now. The fire, it's a portal." It will take her right back to the winter realm, to Lysander's court. It will take a whole chunk of my energy, creating a portal with that destination and propelling them through it, but as long as she and the baby are safe, I don't give a fuck if it costs my life.

"I'm not leaving you," she screams, while the Antichrist's energy whirls towards the ceiling like a growing tornado. It's a matter of minutes until he or she stands in front of me, and even those minutes are a luxury.

Time seems to slow down. Durion rises from his seat with the eyes of a desperate animal about to lose its only prey, Jean Dubois scrambles backwards causing the sofa to tip over, while Antoine shields the twins with his body. Simone backs away with wide eyes as the flames flare.

But before Callie can use her herbs to numb Edith and drag her through the portal, I sense it being hijacked. Foreign yet familiar energy surges through the portal before the visitors take shape from the fire, and step into the room. Damn it! I should have seen this coming because, in the back of my head, I already knew—my time was up.

Sandros

NESSIMA STEPS OUT OF the flames, her eyes burning with betrayal, the creature Killian following.

"Don't look so surprised, Sandros. Certainly, you didn't really expect this plan of yours to work?" she says, squaring her black-clad shoulders like an offended maleficent fairy at a ball she hadn't been invited to. She's wearing her signature all-black fitted dress, looking like a betrayed queen of hell with that creature Killian trailing after her like a big, dumb, ugly-as-fuck but deadly zombie.

If it weren't for Edith, I'd actually be glad she's here. This way I can take all the evil ones to hell with me after I blow this place up.

"What have you done?" Nessima whispers, searching the bright gold in my eyes, and taking a step back. She recognizes hell in them.

"What did you think, Nessima? That I would just let you and the Antichrist take over the world and the Winter Realm?"

"Don't give me that. You deceived me! You made me think you found pleasure in my arms." She shakes as she says it, shoving a finger into my chest. "You're the second man who fucked me over, Sandros. First Eldan, choosing to love a man instead of me, and then you. Putting a glamour on my own creation, having me—" Her mouth twists as she probably relives some of her moments with Killian in her mind. "Who in the cursed realms helped you with this? And don't say you did it all by yourself, because that's just bullshit."

"If you believe Eldan *chose* to love a man instead of loving you, then you deserve everything that happened to you."

"Don't you dare judge me, Sandros."

"Don't you dare talk shit about Eldan. Besides, I've been around long enough to know you chased him like a fucking lunatic, insisted when he didn't show interest."

She presses her lips together, full of rage.

"It's you who refuses to take no for an answer, Nessima. And if you force or manipulate people to do things your way, then expect them to retaliate one way or the other."

I look at Edith for what might be one last time. I was never afraid of war, or battle, or death, or complete destruction for that matter. I *live* for destruction.

But being parted from her, that terrifies me. And with this terror also comes surrender to the truth.

I told myself that my feelings for Edith developed as our bond formed, but now, at what might be the end of my existence, I can't deny it anymore—I've always been crazy about this woman. From the very start, from the moment Lysander placed her under my protection. I wanted her as I sharpened my blade during meetings, watching her from a distance. She took it as a threat, intense dislike, or even the contempt of a fae warlord for his slave. In truth, I was fighting against the attraction that I struggled to keep a lid on and deny. I was hypnotized by her innocent, ethereal looks, and I fucking hated it. She awakened feelings in me that were foreign, new and threatening. I'd been around for centuries, I lived for blood and war, and there she was, a flower on a gloomy battlefield, claiming all of my attention, arresting me with its beauty.

I had to believe she was evil. I had to reject the idea that anything inside her could be good.

Now, she's not only my bonded mate, she's my lifeblood. Through her, I learned that there are many people in the worlds that are worth caring about, such as Callie and the drunkard Antoine who, against all odds, in a situation of extreme stress, proved to have a superior quality of soul. Because there *are* different levels to that. There are good souls. And then there are extraordinary souls.

The power of hell bundles against me, and before I can take on it, I have to get Edith, Callie, the twins and the others out of here. Then I can focus on the Antichrist.

"Here's a battle the great warrior Sandros can't win," Nessima says as she steps back, retribution in her face, her monster flanking her. "This is too big even for you." She points a finger at me. "You shouldn't have gone behind my back. It was one hell of a heist. And you lost."

I stand here, the burning fireplace to my right, watching Nessima and Killian retreat into the darkness that clouds the room. The darkness thickens behind her, rising like a spiral of smoke into the air, spreading over the ceiling.

The Antichrist's power. He or she is behind the woman they've been feeding all this time, finally unfolding. Nessima and Killian step to the side to let the owner of all that power present themselves, a look of wicked satisfaction spreading over Nessima's face.

Then I see him. Yet what hits me hardest isn't his identity, it's the way he magnetizes Edith into his hands with the speed of a lightning bolt. Before I can blink, she's between his claw-like fingers that curl over her upper arms with a hunger to rip her apart. She stares at me with wide eyes, as if she doesn't even realize what's happening yet, not completely.

She's in shock.

He bends his head down over her shoulder, pretending to be whispering in her ear with a grin, but he speaks loud enough for us all to hear.

"If only you'd accepted being mine, Edith."

Durion's eyes meet mine.

"You," I say through my teeth.

"Played my part well, didn't I? A master performance from start to finish." He straightens his back, now towering over the terrified Edith whom he holds like a shield in front of him. The others shrink towards the walls, too terrified to even make a sound.

The mayor tries to scramble out, but Durion's darkness blocks his path like flowing black mist.

"At the queen's birthday," I grit. "You chasing Edith to dance with her, that was all just you scheming?"

He scoffs, as if it's obvious.

"Is that why you came on to her, too?" I demand.

"I came on to her because *you* were into her all along." His features rearrange into a wicked expression, confident, strong, very unlike the Durion Mithriel we'd known until now. Except for the obnoxious part, that stayed the same. "You were crazy about her. What better way to get you exactly where I wanted you if not through her?"

"And where did you want me?"

"Away from Lysander. I hate to admit it, but you and your brother make a dangerous team, even for the forces of hell. And if anything could split you two up, it was her." He caresses Edith's hair, and I lose control. I start toward them, my teeth bared and my eyes blazing, but his darkness shoots in the way and blocks me.

"Don't do that," he snaps, one clawed finger at Edith's throat. "One more move, and she'll be so quickly out of your life you won't believe it."

Edith's wide eyes fix on mine, and anguish grips my heart.

I can't lose her. I can't lose our baby. I would rather die. I *will* die tonight, no doubt about it, because there's no chance in hell I can fight all of this power alone, not with the woman I love in the evil's claws. That fucker has got all the fucking leverage in the world right now. But when I die, I'll be taking him with me if I have to drag him by the balls.

"It all started with a plan," he says, "a plan to defeat the only team that stood a chance to take me down—you and your half-brother, Lysander, the Lord of Winter. But then..." He shifts his attention to Edith again, theatrically, stroking her cheek with the back of his finger. She shivers, her fear a punch in my stomach. "Then you really caught my attention. I even considered, you know, making us a real thing. Maybe I'll still do it. How about we make a deal, yes? I let your lover boy live, and you bind yourself to me for all eternity through a blood oath."

The fires of hell course through me.

A blood oath is unbreakable.

"Over my dead body," I hiss.

"That can be arranged," Durion counters.

"You don't want me, Durion, not really," Edith yelps. "I'm pregnant with Sandros' baby."

If I've ever felt anything close to panic, it's now. What the hell is she thinking?

The expression on Durion's face shifts into one of growing anger, and Nessima's jaw drops. She looks hurt and offended at the same time. Durion is ready to cast Edith aside, and he's ready to do it with enough force to send her hurtling through the wall. I feel him telepathically, through the connection between Edith and me—he wants to kill her, here and now.

"Don't you dare," I warn, the flames rising behind me, spreading out from the fireplace like tongues of fire.

"You care about her more than you care about the world," Durion says, now murderously furious as the darkness rises behind him, ready to take on my flames as the others desperately try to crawl out of the room, screaming and clawing at the closed doors. Their screams are music to Durion and Nessima's ears, especially when Killian moves to pull them back. I have a feeling Nessima has cruel plans for the humans, plans that she intends to implement through Killian, but the bastard is right.

All I care about right now is Edith. I live and breathe for her, and I'm unable to give a fuck about the greater good. She matters more to me than even the baby she carries in her belly, but that's not a good sign. If I stopped caring about the world, the greater good, and even my own baby because I'm consumed by my feelings for a woman, then hell is taking over.

"Let Edith go. This is between you and me," I tell Durion, staring into his eyes.

He measures me up and down, longing to kill me.

"It's me you want."

"Oh, I want her, too."

"You're the fucking Antichrist. Pick on somebody your own size first."

That last one does the job. After a short hesitation, he releases Edith.

"Why the hell not. I can still fuck her after I finish you. I'll fill her expecting womb with my cum."

Rage blasts through my veins, but Edith jumps in front of me, pushing her small hands against my chest, mustering all the strength she's capable of, which isn't much compared to my own.

"Sandros, no," she calls. "He's only going to drag you down with him. Fighting him isn't the way, not like this."

But dragged down with me is exactly where I want him. I want him buried at the bottom of hell, with me as his guardian, making sure he never gets out of there again. Edith tries to lock her arms around me, but I push her out of the way just as the Antichrist attacks. Nessima retreats to the side, cowering by the wall, yet her eyes are set greedily on the fight, greedy to watch my demise.

Durion's darkness rises to push against my flames, muffling the screams behind him. I can't know what's happening there, but I do feel a spark of hope that the twins are protected. It could all end in a bloodbath, and all because of this fucker who played his part so fucking well, blinding me to the truth. Acting the pussy-ass gentlefae was the best cover he could have possibly crafted.

Our powers billow and swell behind us, his darkness like giant waves, my fire like huge tongues of flame. They wrap around us, bringing us close, locking our bodies in a physical struggle.

Physically, I'm stronger, but that doesn't work to my advantage, not in *this* fight. With every fist that crashes into the bastard's face I consume fuel from my fire, while he just takes the hits, laughing, his darkness growing stronger with every blow. A jab at his ribs, the sound of them cracking in my ears, is one more flame that loses itself in the darkness. It doesn't take long until I realize that my superior physical strength and combat skills are the reason I'm losing. But I can't let him get the upper hand either, because I'm already at a disadvantage, and he's sure as fuck not gonna give an ounce of his power away.

So I turn to the last solution. The ace I hoped I wouldn't have to use.

This fight with the Antichrist has always been a battle of strategies. He bested me by having planned this in detail from the start, and having staged everything like a master of deceit all along. I bested him when he thought me safely in Nessima's bed, and I crawled my way out of there, determined to get Edith back. He won by getting us all where he wanted us tonight, and using my own strong suits against me. There's only one thing that I can do now.

"To think that all this time you took me for a weakling," he says, breathing hard, and resting with his hands on his knees. "What did you use to call me? Poet-Face I think, right?" He laughs, a sound like a gritty multitude, grating the humans' ears. They press their hands to the sides of their heads, trying to keep that voice from reverberating in their skulls.

I lower my fists, the only close-combat weapon I could use in this fight. This isn't the kind of conflict that steel or even magic can settle.

"I was wrong about you," I say. "You're not a weakling."

Durion has looked nothing but cocky this whole time, but now a shadow of doubt crosses his eyes.

"You're not even a person," I go on. "You're nothing but a tool. Is this even your body? Have you been Durion Mithriel from the start, or did you have to take possession of his body because you didn't have your own?"

His eyes narrow like a snake's, and I know I'm right. My connection with Edith is still in place, and she has used the battle, and the Antichrist's attention on me, to probe him. Now, she's transferring all of that knowledge to me.

I grin at him as all that information piles up in my head.

"No, you're not a weakling. You're not even a person. But existing in the fae's body, experiencing life through it opened you up to physical experience. You enjoy having feelings. Like desire. Lust. There's something oddly satisfying about experiencing existence in someone's skin, isn't there?" I run my tongue over my teeth, tilting my head to the side. "Too bad you're not actually Durion Mithriel. You're not actually a man. This experience isn't even *really* yours."

Rage spreads out through him as I speak, because I know exactly what buttons to push. I'm fully aware of what my words trigger, and I'm ready to embrace it, knowing that, through my sacrifice, my lover and my baby are going to be safe. The separation from her will be the cauldrons of hell to me, but at least I'm not going down alone. I'm taking Durion with me, making sure he can't hurt them anymore.

It all happens in slow motion, my eyes hanging on Edith's beautiful brown eyes filled with anguish as Durion throws himself at me. He lets out an outcry of rage, arms forward, his darkness hurling itself like black water over my flames. At the last moment I shoot the last of my flames underneath the darkness, wrapping them around the now exposed Durion.

In his rage, he sent everything he had at me, and exposed himself if only for an instant. Now I'm falling through the portal that I created, along with my flames that are wrapped tightly around my nemesis. Nessima and her creature are falling with us, because she is bound to her master, and Killian to his. The portal falls apart above us as we fall with dizzying speed. I burn all bridges, leaving nothing but broken stone and ashes behind.

The Antichrist isn't going to enter the human realm anytime soon, and his horrified face disintegrates right before my eyes as he realizes it.

My hair whips around my face, my clothes ripping from my body from the air friction as we fall until the void catches us, and the Antichrist and I stop face to face. Durion's flesh has been ripped off his bones, and now a bloody angry skull is glaring at me. There's no going back now. I fully embrace the fact that I'll be entangled with him in an endless struggle until the end of time. I'm sure that, with Nessima out of the way, Edith is going to find all the other portals and close them, make sure he's got no more loopholes to sneak in through.

I wonder if she'll be as devastated because of our separation as I am. Even here, on my way to the pits of hell, my feelings for her pulse like a flickering light in my chest, and the Antichrist notices it. Those frayed eyeballs look down at my chest, and it seems that he can see it. I look down, and shock hits. I don't have a body anymore.

It's like....only my mind is here, but not my body.

What in the cursed realms is going on?

A spin starts in what I think is my head, like I'm being sucked into a vortex. I'm swirling upward, through the still falling fire walls of my portal until the vortex spits me out. The portal collapses completely behind me, swallowing the Antichrist's beastly screams that make the walls shudder. He promises retribution.

CHAPTER VI

Sandros

"Lord Sandros! Lord Sandros, are you with us?" a woman's voice echoes through my head. I open my eyes, but I don't recognize the voice nor the face.

But I do recognize Edith when she bends over me, and life surges through my body. I sit up slowly, my head spinning, but I regain my strength fast. Before she knows it, I'm up on my feet, picking her up in my arms as if she were a feather.

"My love," I rasp, pressing my face into her hair, my mouth at her ear. I press her to me, her cool body heating up as we make contact. I realize I might still be carrying the essence of hell with me, since I gave in to my mother's legacy during the battle, and I let Edith go. I can't risk infecting her with it in some way.

But she claws to me and rises on the tips of her toes, her brown eyes glowing with relief and gratitude, her pink lips thirsty for mine. It makes me acutely aware of my own irresistible thirst, so I lean down, cup her head, and press my lips on hers, hard and demanding. Cursed realms, I didn't think I'd ever get to experience this again. She pulls me into her like a magnet, my tongue crazy to feel hers. I must be too much, because she pulls back.

"I'm sorry," I say huskily.

"No, don't be. It's just, we have spectators," she says.

I become aware of the others. I tip my forehead to hers for a moment, not to catch my breath, but to bridle my need to fall inside her and stay there. When I look around the devastated room I'm relieved to see that everyone has survived, even though it doesn't look like they're going to leave this place sane.

Antoine de Auvergne has snapped out of his drunkenness, and is still protecting the children behind him as if he still sees evil everywhere, while Jean Dubois cowers in a corner, hands pressed to his ears like a child escaping the sounds of his parents' screams. Callie is tending to the children behind Antoine, while Simone stands really close to us, her intelligent eyes darting from Edith to me. Looks like she kept her wits about her better than everyone else, but she also seems to be the most ravaged. The 20s diva style waves of her naturally brown hair are disheveled, in fact, she looks like she's just escaped from a street fight.

"What the hell happened to you Mrs. Carrera?" I grit out.

"Mayura."

"Excuse me?"

"My real name isn't Simone Carrera," she says, opening her arms as if giving up on the lies. "I'm Mayura Bogard, and I'm a warrior witch from the Flipside. I was sent here on a mission. Undercover. To help you two."

I keep staring down at her, frowning.

"So your engagement with Antoine," I say. "That's why it didn't make any sense? Because it was only a cover?"

"It was. Poor Guerin, he really wanted that wedding to happen, and I think he genuinely liked me. I felt guilty about him, but I kept telling myself I'd be saving him from the Antichrist, so my lies were good lies." She looks down, her shoulders slouching. "But his soul is now in hell, with the creature he sold it to."

"There are ways to get him back," Edith tries to soothe her, placing a hand on the woman's shoulder. Mayura reacts in that specific way a person reacts when they're sexually attracted to someone, her body tensing, a shade of hope in her eyes. I wind an arm around Edith's waist, pulling her close.

"If you're from the Flipside, then you know what bonded mates are," I say.

Mayura smiles. "Of course. I'm sorry. It's just... your mate is a very special woman."

I press Edith to me tighter.

"She is. Many people will want her, so I better secure my place in her life right now." I look down at Edith just as her eyes snap up to me. She knows where this is going. "I know it's not the time or the place to talk about this, but all this fighting off different admirers is messing with my head." I cup the side of her face. Cursed realms, she's like a small sweet angel in my hands. "As twisted as my feelings for you are Edith, they are love. I love you. Please, marry me."

Callie gasps, and even Antoine is paying attention.

"It's true, he loves you, and that love is what saved his life," Mayura chimes in, drawing my attention.

"For a moment there I thought I wouldn't be able to save him," she tells Edith. "He had fallen fast, and deep to the lowest layers of hell. I'd managed to reach in after them, but my chances of getting him were almost zero. He had gone down with the Antichrist. When one goes to hell, the soul is stripped of anything that could still tie it to the other realms, so that it has nothing to anchor it there. But his love for you still pulsed in his chest like a beacon." She looks up into my eyes, her hostility replaced by some sort of admiration. "I'm in awe with you, Lord Nightfrost. I don't know any other creature that could keep their love burning in the heart of hell. What you feel for Edith, it must be..."

She doesn't have the right words to describe it. But I do.

"It's malignant."

"Which makes it strong as fuck. And it saved the day. It saved your life, and the world."

Edith throws her arms around my waist and pushes her cheek against my chest, her hands slipping under my torn shirt and caressing my scarred body. The wounds are already closing, thanks to my fae nature, but the scars will always be there. I'll always carry the marks of my battles on my skin.

"I love you, too, Sandros. The high realms know I love you so much it hurts."

"She plunged after you through the portal, actually," Mayura says. Panic claws my heart. I grab Edith's shoulders, forcing her to look up at me.

"You did what? Cursed realms, you're pregnant!"

"I wasn't thinking."

"It was a blessing that she did that," Mayura intervenes. "I probably wouldn't have tried to save you otherwise. Edith and the baby were safe, and the Antichrist was going down, thanks to you. The portal was crumbling. My urgent business was now to seal and secure the other portals, not save your life. But after she threw herself I was forced to use my powers, and reach in for her. And then I felt the love pulsing in your chest. It's what enabled me to locate you exactly, and pull you out in the nick of time."

"What kind of a witch are you, by the way?" I inquire.

"I told you, I'm a warrior witch. We work with blood magic and ethereal forces. It's what I used to get you back."

"Ethereal forces?"

"You don't know what those are?"

"I've heard the term thrown around, but that's about it."

She smiles. "Let's just say they allow us warrior witches to change shape, and become anything we want. We can shapeshift into animals, objects, even pure energy, though that's the hardest form to take without dying. It's the highest level in our ranks. I'm a First Class warrior witch."

I give her the semblance of a smile back. "I already like you more."

She laughs.

"I was sent to aid you in finding out who the Antichrist was, which is why I was getting close to Guerin." She glances apologetically at Antoine, who's still too shaken to give a fuck about anything except the kids. I think he sees himself in the boys, on some level. "And it was King Lysander who sent me."

My eyebrow arches up. "My brother?"

Mayura nods. "You managed to get some of Nessima's people on your side at the estate. They wanted back their magic, their powers, so they did everything they could to help you even after you'd gone."

"So my brother knows everything."

"Well not everything." Mayura says. "There are still many things for you to discuss. Much will be changing now, after what happened. The evil must already be lifting from the Blackfall estate and the whole of the North of the Winter Realm, but it will still take a lot of work to bring things back to how they were."

I look at Edith, the woman I could stare at for hours on end.

"We can take care of it. And we will take care of the Snowstorm estate, too. It's been in ruin for too long, and it is time to bring it back to its former glory. *After* the wedding, that is. So, what do you say? Will you—"

"Of course," she says enthusiastically. "Of course I'll marry you!"

She jumps in my arms, her legs swinging around my waist. She presses her soft pink lips to mine, her small hands on my face, her tongue flicking at my lips, wanting to deepen the kiss. Here she is, the love of my life, taking charge. She takes a moment to look into my eyes, her own filling with a happiness that I've never seen in them before. I want to see that happiness every day for the rest of my life.

"You look fantastic in a suit, but I'll have you back in studded leather and mail," she says. "Because that is who you really are—my dark warrior prince."

"That's right. Besides," Mayura throws over her shoulder with a wink, walking away from us. "The Winter King has big plans with the two of you. You'll be needing that studded leather armor, Sandros. So why don't you follow me? It's time to get you two back home."

THE END

SERIES TO BE CONTINUED IN 2022, SO STAY TUNED. YOU WILL BE SEEING MORE OF YOUR FAVORITE CHARACTERS.
Until then, enjoy MORE BOOKS BY ANA CALIN.

Printed in Great Britain
by Amazon